ALSO BY ALEX GINO

George

You Don't Know Everything, Jilly P!

RICK

ALEX GINO

READ WITH **PRIDE**

Alex Gino (signature)

📖 **SCHOLASTIC**

TM & © Scholastic Inc.

For my parents, Cindy and Steve Gino, who transcribed my stories from before I could write and who never once complained that it took three books for me to dedicate one to them.

Library of Congress Cataloging-in-Publication Data available

ISBN 978-1-338-04810-0

3 2021

Printed in the U.S.A. 23
First edition, April 2020

Book design by Maeve Norton

TABLE OF CONTENTS

CHAPTER 1

RICK RAMSEY, RIGHT HAND MAN

Rick Ramsey sat on his bedroom floor on the last day before middle school, spinning quarters. He had just cleaned his room, on his parents' insistence that he start the school year fresh, so the floor was bare except for the rug that looked like a baseball. The whole room was baseball themed, from the time that

Mom and Dad had decided to redecorate just as he signed up for baseball in third grade. Baseball had only lasted eight weeks, but the wallpaper remained.

He chose an especially shiny coin, balanced it between his left thumb and his right middle finger, and set it spinning. He picked up a second and then a third, getting them going as the first tipped from a round-and-round spin to an up-and-down wobble that led to a lie-down flat with a final buzz.

His all-time record was seven quarters moving at once, and that was cutting it close. Most of the time, he could do five. It was harder than it looked. If you didn't give them just the right flick, the coins fell down after a turn or two, or spun under the bed. You had to move fast once the first one was going.

Rick kept spinning until the quarters were scattered around him. Then he scooped them up and began again. This time he put a shiny coin into each hand and spun them both at the same time. The quarter on the right set to dancing on end, while the one on the left started wobbling right away. At least it didn't fall down immediately. When he started practicing simultaneous spins, his right hand produced nothing but wobblers, and his left hand would have gotten more movement by dropping the coin on the table with a plop.

He jumped up when Dad honked the car horn. The car was packed, and Dad was ready to drive Rick's sister, Diane, to her first year of college. Rick dumped the pile of quarters back into their jar and bounded down the stairs and out to the driveway to say goodbye.

"I hope you don't mind that I'm not joining you," Mom said, putting her arm around Diane's shoulder.

"I told you, it's fine! Dad's just going to drop off me and my stuff and then turn right around to go home."

"There's no room for you anyway." Rick was right. The back seat and trunk were filled with crates and bags.

"But we took Thomas out for dinner when he started college."

"I'm not Thomas. Besides, I'm only going an hour away. I'll visit all the time."

"I'll still miss you," said Mom.

"I'll miss you too," said Diane, as though it were a challenge. They entangled in a mess of long straight black hair and pale pink limbs. Dad joined in with his thicker, hairier arms and wavy light brown hair, and called Rick into the family huddle. Rick had Dad's hair and Mom's skin tone, but sometimes, like most kids, he wondered where he had come from.

Rick and Diane exchanged a series of high fives and high tens before Diane enveloped him in her arms. "Promise you won't grow up on me while I'm gone."

"Uh . . ." Rick had no plans on growing up before her first visit home in three weeks, but it seemed like a weird thing to promise.

"Promise me!"

"Diane." Dad put a heavy hand on Rick's shoulder. "Rick's about to start middle school. Whole new worlds are opening up for him. Girls . . ."

"Or boys," added Mom.

"Point is, the two of you are on new journeys and we're proud of you both."

Rick didn't really think there was much of a comparison. There would be plenty of kids at middle school he had known for years, especially his best friend, Jeff. Girls, or boys, were nothing new. Changing classes sounded like fun, but he didn't get to pick them the way Diane did. And at the end of every day, he would still be coming home to the same house, just with one less person in it.

Mom embraced Dad and said, "Drive safe, Robbie."

"Always," said Dad, kissing Mom on the lips. "Okay, give your mom one more hug, Diane, and let's get out of here."

Rick and Mom waved as the car drove away.

Neither of them moved from the sidewalk until it had reached the light three blocks down and turned out of sight.

"Well, two down, one to go, I guess," said Mom with a smile propped on her face.

"Hey, Mom, is it okay if I go to Jeff's?"

Jeff had instant messaged the night before that he had gotten the new *Barfight 3000* and that Rick should come over.

"And leave me with a quiet home to take a nap in?" said Mom. "By all means, my little dove. Just be home by seven for dinner. And come give your Mama Bird a hug before you go."

Rick leaned over, and Mom kissed him on the forehead. It felt kind of wet, but he didn't rub it off.

He grabbed his bike out of the shed and pedaled over to Jeff's place. Rick and Jeff had been best friends since the second week of third grade, when Rick had done an impression of Mrs. Fields, the old woman who volunteered in the lunchroom, and Jeff had laughed so hard milk had come out of his nose. Neither of them had known that could really happen, and that made them laugh even harder. Rick hadn't had a whole lot of friends, and Jeff was new, and soon they were a molecule, Jeff-n-Rick. Rick liked being part of a molecule.

That spring, when Rick signed up for baseball, Jeff signed up too. Two months later, when Rick admitted he was having a terrible time, Jeff quit right alongside him. And when Dad told Rick it was important to take on a challenge, Jeff had pointed out that video games were just as challenging as physical sports and just as good for hand-eye coordination, with none of the risk of being hit by a flying lump of rubber, yarn, and cowhide.

Sometimes Jeff didn't think before he spoke, or before he acted, especially when he didn't like something. But Jeff liked hanging out with Rick, and

Rick liked hanging out with Jeff, and sometimes that was all you needed to be best friends.

Jeff's little green two-story house had a steeply sloped red attic that looked like the letter *A* and a pair of pink rosebushes by the front door. Jeff's mom, Stacey, met Rick at the door and welcomed him in. She was tall, like Jeff, with thick lines on her face and her hair back in a messy bun. She wore black yoga pants and a gray tank top with faded writing that said, *I've already done my good deed for the day. Try again tomorrow.*

"C'mon up!" Jeff called from upstairs.

"You heard him—go do your thing," Stacey said with an offhand wave.

Rick ran up the wide first flight, then climbed more slowly as the stairs narrowed and turned in on themselves.

Jeff's room was the entire attic, so it was big, but the ceiling sloped down so you could only stand up in the middle of the room. Old boxes and suitcases ran along the two long-but-low walls. A mattress with messy black sheets and a single pillow took up one corner. A worn wooden bureau with the top drawer pulled out and sitting on the floor was centered on the third wall, below a round window that opened outward. The fourth wall was mostly the staircase. A flat-screen TV sat on the floor in the middle of the room, flanked by stacks of video games and in front of two black leather beanbag chairs.

Jeff was already in one of the beanbag chairs, controller in hand and screen paused. His face was peachy white, with a small white scar on his forehead and short brown hair that stuck up like loose spikes. He wore red basketball shorts and a black sleeveless T-shirt.

"This game is awesome. You can actually crack a bottle on a guy's head and the shards embed in his skull."

"Lemme see!" Rick dropped into the empty chair.

Jeff pressed a series of buttons, and a hulking character on the screen picked up a bottle that read *XXX* and cracked it over the skull of a skinny little guy drinking at the bar.

"Aww man!" Jeff groaned. "None of them stuck that time! Here, you take the other controller and I'll restart the game."

"Won't you have to do everything over?" asked Rick.

"Dude, it's a bar brawl. Who cares?"

That was one of the cool things about Jeff—he didn't really care about things like high scores and winning streaks. Rick's older brother, Thomas, *never* restarted a video game to let Rick join in. In fact, sometimes, he used to leave a game paused for days because he was between save points on his quest and didn't want to have to retrace his steps. Rick wasn't allowed to play anything on the game system until Thomas was done.

Now Rick and Jeff re-entered the game's bar—a blinking neon sign told Rick it was named The Rampage. The brawl was already going, so the two of them had to take on every hostile customer they encountered. Rick even managed to get some glass to stick to a woman's head, which got him a midgame high five from Jeff. They threw punches, kicks, and bottles until the room was empty and the bartender officially put their faces up on the Barred-Entry Wall of Fame list.

Jeff checked out his window. "Looks like Gene's gone. Let's go downstairs and get some soda." Gene was Jeff's dad. Stacey was nice. Gene was . . . well, Stacey was nice, anyway.

Stacey appeared in the doorway of the kitchen while Jeff was pouring two large cups of orange soda. "So, Rick, you excited about middle school?"

"I guess."

"I have to keep reminding this one over here that

it's not going to be like fifth grade." Stacey tipped her head toward Jeff.

Jeff grunted. "I know, Mom."

"There are going to be more responsibilities—"

"And more opportunities to get in trouble," Jeff finished Stacey's song of the summer.

"I'm glad you're aware. Now make sure you find those opportunities and *avoid them*." Stacey turned to Rick. "You'll make sure he stays out of trouble, right?"

"I'll try?" Rick stared at the streams of bubbles in his cup, wishing this conversation weren't happening. If he had raised his eyes, he would have seen that Jeff looked at least as uncomfortable.

"Mom," Jeff said, "this is our last day before middle school, and we just want to relax."

"Fine, fine," said Stacey. "I'm not here to give you a hard time. But if you get into trouble, you'll learn new meanings of the word *punishment*."

"Mom, when have I ever been in trouble?"

"You got into two fights last year!"

"Yeah, but neither of them was my fault. Right, Rick?"

Rick tried to sink into his chair. The way Jeff told it, nothing was ever his fault. And really, Jeff was right about the one kid at the park who had freaked out because he thought Jeff had stolen his bike, when it turned out they just had the same model. But with Evan at school, it had totally been Jeff who'd turned it into a fight. And he had punched a kid in fourth grade too, though that hadn't turned out well for him.

"It *was* your bike." Rick hated lying, but he also hated having people mad at him. It was best when he could come up with a way to say the truth that left out the parts someone might not want to hear.

"Just do your best to stay out of trouble, okay?" Stacey said.

"I will. C'mon, Rick, let's go." Jeff grabbed his soda and headed for the stairs. Rick followed, glad both to get away from the conversation and that he hadn't been the one to end it.

"Sorry about my mom," Jeff said once they were back upstairs. "I was so worried about not running into the Dad-odile that I forgot the Mom-opotamus is the most dangerous creature on the Great Orange Soda River."

"Especially on the day before school starts, when the parental beasts of the suburban savannah are most likely to pounce."

"No kidding. So, what should we play now?" Jeff gestured at his pile of video games.

"What if we work on Nohomeworksburg? We're only fifty thousand civilians from a major disaster."

Rick and Jeff had been playing *VirtualTown* all summer, and they had read online that once their town of Nohomeworksburg reached a population of one million, it would be hit by either a hurricane, an earthquake, wildfires, or Godzilla. Rick and Jeff were hoping for Godzilla.

"I could go for that," said Jeff.

Rick smiled. He loved when Jeff approved of his choices. Sometimes Rick pictured himself as Alexander Hamilton, like in that musical Mom loved, and Jeff was General George Washington. Not that Jeff was anything like the first United States president, but there was this song about Hamilton being his right-hand man, and sometimes Rick felt like that. Jeff wasn't a general, or twenty-five years older than him, and he had never crossed the Delaware River in a rowboat, but he *did* know how to navigate a room full of kids. And with the choppy waters of sixth grade only seventeen hours away, that could be more important than ever.

CHAPTER II

SHE DOESN'T USE THAT
NAME ANYMORE

Rick had a tough time falling asleep that night and an even tougher time waking up in the morning. He ignored his alarm through three snooze cycles, until Mom burst into his room and yanked the curtains wide open.

"Too bright!" Rick grumble-yelled.

"You have no idea how gentle I am. My mom would tear that blanket right off your warm and comfy body. Now, get up!"

Rick rolled his eyes, then rolled his body out of bed. He was dressed and in the kitchen before the Mom alarm went off again. Four corn muffins remained in a baking tin on the stove with a note from Dad that said, *Good Luck, Rick!* Rick arranged three into a triangle on a plate, poured a glass of iced tea, and sat down at the kitchen table to slather the muffins in butter.

"Glad to see you up." Mom came back into the kitchen and swiped the last corn muffin off the stovetop. "I'll drive you to school in ten minutes."

"What? Why?" Now that Rick was in middle school, he would be taking the city bus, just like Diane and Thomas had before him. "I know where the bus stops."

"You'd have to leave right now to catch it. You can

take the bus home. Let me have these last few moments before I have a kid who's old enough to take public transportation all on his own."

"I'm not going to be any older at three o'clock than I am right now." Technically, he would be about seven hours older, but Rick decided it was more important to make a point than be accurate.

"Hush and let me live my fantasy."

Ten minutes later, Rick was buckled into the passenger's seat of Mom's bright yellow Beetle. He even let Mom give him a hug when they got to school, but he was glad she didn't try to kiss him on the cheek the way moms did on television shows to embarrass kids. Rick had already spotted Jeff waiting for him on the other side of the fence, and Jeff at school wasn't the same as Jeff without other kids around. When it was just the two of them, nothing really bothered Jeff. But in a group, he was always on the lookout for something to make fun of.

Or lately, to stare at, if there was a girl he deemed pretty. This morning, it was a girl.

"Check out the hottie!" Jeff said in greeting. He tossed his head vaguely across the schoolyard.

"Which one?" Rick hated when Jeff called girls hotties. He made it sound like they were sexy pancakes.

"Right there." Jeff pointed. "In the blue skirt."

All Rick could tell about the girl standing on the far side of the yard was that she was white, had a short haircut, and wore a pink shirt with a blue skirt. She was deep in animated conversation with a light-skinned Black kid with a buzzed head, jeans, and a black T-shirt with the image of a giant pair of open scissors on the back.

"Yeah, I'd like to see more of her, if you know what I mean." Jeff elbowed Rick in the ribs. Rick knew what Jeff meant, and Jeff knew that Rick knew what he meant, but Jeff continued anyway. "With her clothes off."

Rick gave what he hoped was enough of a laugh.

"You know," said Jeff, "I saw a lady walking around on the beach without her clothes this summer."

"You told me. You sure she wasn't just wearing a bathing suit the color of her skin?"

"No, dude, I told you! She was super naked. And hot too. Everyone was staring. Men, women, kids. Even the fish."

Rick gave another expected laugh, but before Jeff could tell him any more about the beach show, the school doors opened and a graceful but firm woman wearing a deep purple suit jacket stepped outside with a bullhorn. She pressed the whooping alarm button twice and the crowd of students turned to face her, their conversations trailing off into whispers.

"Welcome, everyone. I'm Principal Baker. I hope each and every one of you had an enjoyable and relaxing summer. You should have received a letter listing your homeroom, which is where you will head now. If you have forgotten your homeroom, or did not get your letter, there are lists posted inside the building. Please enter carefully and quietly, and I wish you all a wonderful start to the school year."

The students closest to the doors started to shuffle inside while the mass behind them crowded in on the school. The sea of students pushed forward, closer and closer together, until Rick made it through to the wide hallway, and then into the packed stairwell and up to the third floor, where large signs listing classroom numbers directed students to the left or right.

He turned to say *see ya* to Jeff, but Jeff had slipped several people ahead and was already going down the hall in the other direction. Jeff didn't like good-byes, not even when you would see each other again in a few hours.

Rick checked the numbers painted above the classroom doors until he was standing in front of room 326. This was it, the official start of middle school. "Come on!" groaned a kid behind him, and Rick stepped into the classroom. It was slightly chillier than the hallway, and much brighter. A woman with large, bouncy curls of chestnut hair stood at the front of the room. She looked too young and too happy to be a middle school teacher, but there she was, her name written on the whiteboard in large capital letters: *MS. MEDINA.*

Rick stood next to a group of boys who were too involved in a picture one of them was sketching to notice him. The bell rang and a few last kids ended their hallway conversations and dashed into the room.

Ms. Medina held a sheet of paper in her hand and stood at the desk in the corner. "As I call your name, please come take your seat quietly. Annie Allen," she began, and a short girl with white-blonde hair made her way up to the desk at the front of the room.

"Basil Chan, Alia Damon, David Delgado." Ms. Medina made her way down the desks in a line, calling out the names of the students who were to occupy them.

"Melissa Mitchell." The girl with the blue skirt was the first student in the third row. Ms. Medina kept calling out names. At the start of the next row, Rick was assigned to the desk immediately behind Melissa.

Once everyone was seated, Ms. Medina gave out class schedules along with a speech about the importance of starting middle school on the right foot and making time each day not only to complete your assignments but also to keep on top of what lay in store for the following days and weeks.

"The bell to move to first period will ring in a few minutes. In the meantime, I want you to turn to someone near you, *quietly* introduce yourself, and tell them one thing you're excited for this year."

The kid on Rick's left turned to his left, and the kid behind him had turned to the kid behind her, so Rick was glad to see the girl with the blue skirt turn back and wave.

"Hi." He gave a small wave back. "I'm Rick."

"I know." Melissa smiled with a mix of nerves and glee.

And that's when Rick realized that the girl in the blue skirt was no stranger. He had gone to school with her since first grade. He even used to play checkers with her, before he and Jeff had become best friends.

"Wait, is that you, G—?"

Melissa stopped him with a raised finger as well as her voice. "I don't use that name anymore. You can call me Melissa."

"Oh. Um, hi."

"Yeah, hi."

They sat there for a moment in the din of introductions, just seeing each other.

"You look good." Rick meant it. Not the way Jeff would, but more like she looked happy. Last year, her hair had been in her face and her eyes were almost always focused on the ground. Now her reddish-brown hair was brushed back and her eyes were looking right at Rick.

"Thanks."

Rick's brain felt like a vacuum, and the next words that came to his mind popped right out of his mouth. "So you're . . ."

"I'm a girl. A transgender girl. I wanted to come to school as myself last year, but my mom said I should wait for a fresh start in middle school."

"That makes sense, I guess."

Melissa shrugged. "It would have been nice to stop hiding sooner."

"That makes sense too." Rick gave a small, awkward smile. He would have thought it would be weird to meet a transgender girl, but it wasn't, really. At least, not if the girl was Melissa. He continued, "So I guess I know what you're excited about this year."

Melissa laughed. "Nervous too, but mostly excited. What about you?"

"I dunno. The regular stuff, I guess. Changing classes sounds kinda fun."

"Yeah," said Melissa. "Wanna see my binder?"

Melissa brought out a purple binder that she had drawn intricate geometric designs on in permanent marker. Rick brought out his, which was plain black but had already been set up with each class assigned a color tab—red for math, yellow for Spanish, blue for English.

When the bell rang, the room devolved into a whirl of chaos. Rick found himself right behind Melissa in the rush to the door, where the kid who had been next to Melissa in the yard waited, bouncing in place. From the front, her T-shirt read, *WARNING: RUNS WITH SCISSORS.*

"I missed you!" The kid practically pounced on Melissa.

"Kelly, homeroom was fifteen minutes long."

"A person could drown in fifteen minutes!"

And then they were gone, arm in arm, heading down the hallway and exclaiming over each other's schedules.

Rick wondered what it would be like to have a best friend you could throw your arm over the shoulder of without worrying that they might make fun of you. Jeff was great in a lot of ways, but their friendship wasn't like that. Nor was Jeff the kind of friend who wanted to hear that a person could, in fact, drown nearly four times in fifteen minutes, assuming a standard of four minutes from first struggle to death from lack of oxygen to the brain. When Rick corrected stuff like that, Jeff told him not to think so hard.

Rick didn't see Jeff again until lunch. In between,

he had been to three different classes with three different teachers and been assigned four different seats to remember, including homeroom. His mind was swirling, and his backpack was heavy with textbooks. By then, the idea that George could be a girl seemed a bit less sensible, and the idea that it would freak Jeff out because he had talked about whether she was cute was a bit more appealing.

"Remember that girl in the blue skirt from this morning?"

"You mean the *hot* one?"

"Yeah, well, she sits in front of me in homeroom, and I found something out . . ."

"How was she close up?"

But then Melissa's smile from this morning passed across Rick's mind and his stomach burbled and it didn't feel at all exciting to tell Jeff that she was the same kid he had bullied for years.

"I dunno. Fine, I guess."

"You gotta pay more attention. I mean, you've gotta notice a good butt when it's sitting right in front of you. Sometimes, it's like I have to explain everything to you. So, what'd you find out?"

Rick hesitated. "Just that her name is Melissa."

"So?"

"I thought you might want to know."

"Dude, I don't need her name. I need info I can *use*. Does she have anything up here?" Jeff brought his hands up to his chest.

Rick shrugged. He didn't want to think about Melissa like that. "Her voice is nice."

Jeff eyed Rick with a note of disappointment. "Whatever. There are hotter girls around."

"But you were the one who said she . . ." Rick was too flabbergasted to finish his sentence.

"Don't get caught in a web of details, Rick. The point is, we're in middle school now. We don't need to get hung up on one girl."

If there was one thing that made less sense to Rick than the way Jeff knew someone was cute, it was the way Jeff knew he wasn't all that interested anymore. It was like he had a switch he could turn on and off whenever he chose, like it was a lamp or something.

The whole *liking people* thing was a complete mystery to Rick. And he wasn't about to ask Jeff to explain it.

After school, Rick grabbed a handful of quarters from his jar and sat on the living room floor. Twirling Washingtons was relaxing, and he was getting good at a new trick of stopping the quarter mid-spin with the pad of his finger. When he lifted the finger, the coin would stay on its side, at least some of the time.

Rick was still practicing when Dad came in from his garage office, where he worked as a general contractor.

"Hey, bud," Dad said. "How was the first day of middle school?"

"Exhausting. By the time we each got an assigned seat and a textbook in one class, it was practically time to get back up again. Then we had to search around for the next classroom, where we had to stand against the walls and do it all over again."

"And just think, soon you'll be complaining about homework and tests and wishing all you had to do was stand around and get your textbooks."

"Thanks, Dad. That really cheers me up."

"It couldn't have all been bad. Were there any cute girls?"

Rick shrugged. "Yeah, I guess. I was too busy trying to find my classes."

"Oh, trust me, Ricky, you're never too busy to take a look at a girl." Sometimes Dad was worse than Jeff. "Or a boy." Mom probably told him to say that part. "You may be a late bloomer, but don't worry, you'll have plenty of time to take in the views, if you know what I mean."

Rick knew what Dad meant, and it made him feel like he was coated in a sticky layer of ick. He didn't even have homework as an excuse to get out of the conversation. "I'll look around tomorrow. I promise."

"I believe in you, bud." Dad laughed.

Rick hadn't meant it to be funny. "Thanks, Dad."

"Alright, then. I gotta put in another hour before I can call it quits for the day." Dad grabbed a can of soda from the fridge and headed back to the garage.

Rick pulled up an old episode of *Extreme Calligraphers' Challenge. ECC* was a public television show that was pretty much what it sounded like. Rick and Diane had gotten hooked on the first episode and couldn't get enough of the swirling cursive lettering and the goofy banter between the competitors and the host. This was the one when C. J. lost the semifinal competition because he misspelled one of the judges' names. Ever since, "pulling a C. J." meant really messing something up.

Rick was pretty sure his *liking*-people neurons were pulling a C. J. At least C. J. got to leave the show and return to the real world, where no one cared what his calligraphy skills were like. Rick had to keep pretending and deflecting while everyone, even his father, seemed to think he should turn into some sort of hormonal beast now that he was in middle school.

Rick wished Diane was still around. Not even to talk to, but just to be there. If Diane were home, she would make popcorn and Rick would load up the latest episode of *Extreme Calligraphers' Challenge*.

She wouldn't ask Rick about hot girls, and if he liked any of them.

That, Rick thought, would be a big relief.

CHAPTER III

ICE CREAM EITHER WAY ISN'T A BAD DEAL

"If Grandpa Ray wants to talk to people, why doesn't he just go out and make friends?"

Rick sat in the passenger seat of Dad's car on Sunday. They were on the way to the big block of a building where Grandpa Ray lived, with its criss-cross mowed lawn, green bushes that lined the walkway to the front door, and a sign hanging from the second floor that read *Sunrise Apartments. Rooms Available.* There were always rooms available at Sunrise Apartments.

"Grandpa Ray has friends," said Dad. "But sometimes grandparents like to receive visits from their grandchildren, and today the torch has been passed on to you."

Rick's older brother, Thomas, started visiting Grandpa Ray in high school as something to write about on his college applications. When he started college, Diane took his place. And now, Rick had inherited the position. Rick had messaged Diane that morning to ask what her meetings with Grandpa Ray used to be like, but he hadn't heard back.

Grandpa Ray was an okay guy, but Rick had mostly seen him at holidays and birthdays, where Grandpa Ray pretty much sat in a corner, listening to the other adults talk. Rick and Grandpa Ray had never said much more than a few sentences to each other at once.

"It's gonna be so boring. What are we even going to say for two and a half hours? I don't think we've talked that long combined in our entire lives."

"Well, you can always tell him about your first week at school."

Rick groaned. Going to school was bad enough without having to run through it all over again. Homework from a legion of teachers was already worse than homework from one.

"Dad's quiet in large groups, but I know you'll like him once you get to know him more one-on-one. Thomas and Diane always had a great time. Maybe he'll show you some pictures of your Grandma Rose."

Grandma Rose had died six months before Rick was born, which meant that he was the only member of his family who had never met her. Rick thought it was weird to call a person he had never met *Grandma*, but that's how adults were. Rick didn't want to look at photos of a dead person, and he really didn't want to spend the afternoon listening to stories about one.

"If he's so great, why don't *you* spend the afternoon with him?"

"I see him for coffee on Thursdays. Today, I'm going back home to spend a kid-free afternoon with your mother."

"But—"

"Don't make me pull The Parent Card. You're going. There's more to your Grandpa Ray than you know. He's led a full life and has a lot of interests. I'm sure you'll find something to connect over. There's plenty about him I still don't know myself."

Rick crossed his arms and would have full-on

sulked, but the trip to Sunrise Apartments was so short that Dad was already turning onto the block before he could work up a good one.

"Tell you what, bud. If you have a terrible time, we'll pick up ice cream on the way home."

"Does that mean I don't get ice cream if I have a good time? That's not fair."

"Fine. We'll stop at Robin's either way."

Rick grinned. It was hard to be upset knowing that two scoops of triple chocolate fudge with chocolate sprinkles were just hours from partying in his mouth.

At the heavy metal-and-glass door, Rick pressed the button for apartment 4E. Moments later the door buzzed and the lock released, letting him into an airy lobby with a marble mantel under a large mirror, and an old, intricate ironwork banister leading up a set of stairs. The door to the left of the stairs had a diamond-shaped window that opened into the darkness of an elevator shaft. He pressed the button and a machine below hummed, clacked, and rattled until the diamond window of the door lined up with the diamond window of the elevator. Then it stopped and Rick waited until he realized he would need to open the door himself.

Rick had been to Grandpa Ray's building plenty of times to pick him up on the way to visit his cousins with Mom and Dad, but he couldn't remember ever going up to the apartment before. He held his breath and counted the diamonds of light as the small window passed the door on each floor, thankful that the lobby already counted as the first. *Ka-thunk-a-chunka-creak.* Two. *Bumpa-bumpa-bumpa-bumpa-rattttttle.* Three. *Scheee-screee-schreeech-boomp.* Four.

Rick exhaled with relief as he pushed open the door and stepped out into the hallway. Grandpa Ray was waiting at the door of his apartment and waved Rick inside. He was stocky, with tufts of bright white hair, a full face, and an even fuller smile.

"Welcome to my bachelor pad!" Grandpa Ray flourished his hand palm-up around his one-room apartment.

"It's nice," Rick replied, hoping he sounded like he meant it.

"It's cozy and it's all mine. There's my kitchen"—he gestured at a small stove, a mini-fridge, and a sink lined up along one wall—"and this is the dining room." He pointed at a table in the corner. "The living room." A couch across from a television. "This here's the library." A bookcase. "And of course, the bedroom suite." Grandpa Ray turned to the bed that filled one corner of the room, its sheets perfectly flat, with a blanket folded like an accordion at the foot.

It all looked fine to Rick, even if a single bookcase wasn't much of a library. He sensed Grandpa Ray wanted him to say something more than *It's nice*, though, so he blurted out the only words that landed in his brain. "I hate making my bed. I'm just going to mess it up the next day."

Grandpa Ray laughed. "Any other day of the week, and that bed would be a pile of blankets and pillows. But I change the sheets and make the bed every Sunday. Rose used to do that, and I don't want her haunting me over some linens, like some kind of Bzork."

"What did you just say?" Rick turned his head so fast his neck hurt.

"I don't want Rose to Bzorkava me into a canister of Braxyl & Sons Ultra Goo. And shut your mouth unless you want a Tseel to fly in!"

"I didn't know you watched *Rogue Space*!"

"Who doesn't watch *Rogue Space*?" Grandpa Ray shrugged innocently, but his eyes sparkled and his lips hinted at a smile.

"My parents don't."

"I tried my hardest with your dad, but he was a lost cause. And your mom, well, she's one of the smartest people I've ever met, but I've never seen her watch anything that took more than about three brain cells to follow the plot of, if you know what I mean."

"My best friend, Jeff, says only geeks and idiots watch *Rogue Space*."

"Your best friend, Jeff, doesn't have a clue what he's talking about. Geeks and idiots have very different television habits. Forget about that kid. Have you seen *The Smithfield Specials*?"

Rick shook his head. He had never heard of them. Grandpa Ray explained that they were a series of four movie-length episodes that had never aired on television due to legal disputes. They were filmed in 1997–98, the only two years in the last thirty that *Rogue Space* wasn't on the air in some form.

"The special effects weren't what they are today, but *The Smithfield Specials* give some pretty amazing backstory into why the Bzorki and the Garantula hate each other so much, and the dialogue is sharp! And it just so happens I have the complete collection. What do you say?"

"That sounds awesome!" said Rick. "But Dad said I was here to talk with you."

"You're here for a fun visit. And what could be more fun than *Rogue Space*?"

"Not much. But Grandpa Ray, I've known you my whole life. How did I never know you were a Roguer?"

"Did you ever ask?" Grandpa Ray raised a bushy gray eyebrow along with the corner of his lips.

From the first *nah-duh* of the theme song, watching *Rogue Space* with Grandpa Ray was way more fun than watching it alone. Grandpa Ray started humming the tune, and Rick joined in, and they took turns shouting the *zoom*s and *deedle*s that coursed through the intro. Together they gave a great *"BOOM!"* and whispered "rogue spaaaaaaaaaaace" until the words faded and a Garantulan face filled the screen.

The special effects were kind of bad, but the episode explained why the Bzorki left their home planet, which was something Rick had always wondered. When the words *TO BE CONTINUED . . .* lingered on the television screen, Rick asked whether they could start episode two.

"You know your dad's going to be here soon to pick you up, right?"

"Already?" Rick exclaimed.

"I told you they were movie-length episodes."

"Yeah, but it went by so fast!"

"You were expecting the time with your Grandpa Ray to drag."

"No," said Rick. "I mean . . ."

"It's okay," said Grandpa Ray. "You had every

reason to be nervous. We haven't really hung out before, just us. For all you knew, it could have been like spending two hours with your dad."

Rick laughed.

Grandpa Ray went on. "So, what are you going to tell that friend of yours about watching *Rogue Space* with your Grandpa Ray? You know, the one who hates us Roguers?"

"He doesn't hate us. He just doesn't get it."

"Well, are you going to say anything to him about it?"

"No." Rick shrugged.

"Interesting," said Grandpa Ray. "Is that how you usually handle conflicts with him?"

"We don't really fight," said Rick. It was true. That was one of the things Jeff said he liked about Rick.

"Sounds like you don't give him anything to fight about," Grandpa Ray pointed out.

"Isn't that a good thing?"

"You'd think so, wouldn't you?"

Rick wished he were the kind of person who asked questions in moments like this. But he wasn't, and he didn't. Instead he and Grandpa Ray dropped into silence. A comfortable silence, though, just sitting next to each other on the couch and thinking about everything and nothing at once.

Grandpa Ray jumped when his phone buzzed, and that made Rick jump too.

"Your dad's downstairs."

"Can we watch another *Smithfield Special* next week?"

"I sure hope so!" Grandpa Ray said as he gave Rick a hug. "And Rick?"

"Yeah?"

"Think carefully about who you spend time with. The right people? Well, they can bring you great joy."

"And the wrong people bring sadness?"

Grandpa Ray shook his head. "Not even.

Sometimes the right people bring sadness too. The wrong people are the ones who keep you from being yourself."

"Uh, okay," said Rick.

"We'll talk next week." And with that, Grandpa Ray held the door open for Rick, who skipped the elevator and jogged down the four flights of stairs in a twist of right turns and echoes.

"So, bud, are we going out for ice cream or for ice cream?" Dad asked when Rick got into the car.

"What?"

"You know . . . ice cream?" Dad smiled goofily and gave two thumbs-up. "Or ice cream?" He threw his head back in boredom and his thumbs down.

"Ice cream!" Rick gave a thumbs-up and a much less goofy smile. "Why didn't you tell me he likes *Rogue Space*?"

"Oh, that's right. He and your grandma used to

watch it every week. Your aunt Ruby and I, we never got into it, but your grandpa is a real Roguer. So, what kind of ice cream are you getting? Chocolatey chocolate with a side of chocolate?"

"What else is there?"

"Oh gosh. There are all sorts of great flavors. Take rum raisin, for instance. For years, I thought I hated it. I mean, it just doesn't *sound* like an ice cream flavor. But then I was thinking about it one day, and I realized: I like raisins. I like rum. I like ice cream. What's the problem? I tried it, and now it's one of my favorites."

Dad sounded proud of his own wisdom, whatever it meant. He turned on the radio to a baseball game. Rick didn't care about the game or the score, but it made for comforting background noise as he let his mind wander to what it would be like to grow up with parents who watched *Rogue Space* with him. Or to have a best friend who didn't make fun of the show.

A few batters later, Dad pulled into a spot right in front of Robin's Marvelous Cups & Cones. There were only eight people in line in front of them. Not bad for a Sunday afternoon. With three people serving up ice cream, the wait wouldn't be long at all. Rick recognized the three of them from past visits, and they were all experts at scooping, stacking, and sprinkling.

Soon he was standing across the freezer from Mo, Rick's all-time favorite server. A line of earrings ran up her left ear, and today her ponytail was black with blue highlights.

"The usual?" she asked.

"You know it!" said Rick, and Mo prepared a cup with two scoops of triple chocolate fudge and loaded the top with chocolate sprinkles. Dad ordered a cone with one scoop of rum raisin and one of espresso.

"So, you enjoying middle school so far?" Dad asked once they settled in at a small, round white table outside the shop.

"I guess."

"How's getting from one class to the next?" Dad took a lick of his cone.

"It's okay."

"Been making new friends?"

"A couple."

"Middle school is a great time. It can also be a pain in the neck, but it's a great time. You're growing up, becoming more independent, turning into a real person, you know?"

"Sort of."

"Do you ever use more than two words at a time?" Dad asked.

"Not really," said Rick, which made Dad laugh his infectious, gigglesnort laugh, until Rick broke and laughed too, in his high *hee-hee-heee*.

Rick ate a big spoonful of ice cream, and his mind turned back to Grandpa Ray. Hanging out with him was way more comfortable than Rick had been expecting it to be. Easier than hanging out with Dad. And fun. Rick had never heard Grandpa Ray talk about *Rogue Space* before. Rick hadn't heard him say that much about anything before. It was almost as if Grandpa Ray felt more comfortable with Rick than he expected too. Rick could barely wait for next Sunday.

CHAPTER IV

PLATO WAS GAY, EVEN DURING SCIENCE CLASS

School kept schooling along into a second week. It wasn't terrible, but it also wasn't terribly exciting. Rick could remember where all of his classes were, and he even knew which one to go to when without looking at the paper in his binder. He didn't have any classes with Jeff, but they saw each other in the morning and at lunch, and Rick was getting to know a few kids in his homeroom who he shared a bunch of his classes with.

Thursday morning, Rick got dressed, ate breakfast, and took the bus to school, with its twists and turns that sent him flying if he wasn't holding on tight. He laughed with Jeff in the schoolyard about what would happen if all of the teachers turned into dogs and came running out of the school and everyone played fetch and tug-the-stick all day long. And in homeroom, Ms. Medina let them do what they wanted quietly as long as they stayed in their seats and didn't disrupt her taking attendance.

Rick pulled out a quarter and practiced one-handed spins, stopping the coin on its side with his fingertip. First with his right hand, to warm up, and then with his left.

"That's really cool. How do you do it?" Melissa asked, surprising Rick. Melissa had smiled at him before, but this was the first time that she had spo-ken to him since the first day of school.

"You have to be really careful," said Rick. "If you press too hard the coin falls over."

"Can I try?"

"Sure." Rick gave her his quarter. He showed her how to hold the coin between her thumb and her pointer finger, with the edge a millimeter above her desk. Then with a twist of her fingers, she let go of the coin. It wobbled for a moment and then lay still.

"It's easier to get them going with two hands," said Rick, demonstrating by balancing the coin between his two pointer fingers, "but if you mess up, it could go shooting across the room."

Melissa looked up at Ms. Medina, who was still scanning the class and marking off students in her attendance book. "That sounds like a bad idea."

"No kidding."

Melissa tried again, and this time, the coin didn't

even wobble. It just fell flat. Rick pulled out another coin, set it spinning on end, and then stopped it with the pad of his finger.

"How do you even *do* it?"

"Practice. And watch this." But when Rick released his finger, the coin toppled over.

"Oh, that I can do!" Melissa stood the coin on its end with her finger and let go so that the coin fell. Rick smiled. Then she did it again. And again. "See? I'm an expert!"

Rick started to laugh, and Melissa joined in, each chuckle reminding the other how funny it was. Both laughed into their hands until Ms. Medina looked their way, and they stared at the ground to try to gain their composure.

That afternoon, Rick arrived in Mr. Vincent's science class and opened to the green tab in his binder. Mr. Vincent was a thin white man with a thick, dark mustache and a receding hairline. He wore an orange button-down shirt with thin white stripes and an orange tie with white polka dots. Rick thought he couldn't have looked more like a middle school science teacher if he'd tried. He seemed like the kind of guy who measured his raisin bran and milk in the morning, not because he was on a diet, but because he wanted to get the perfect ratio of crunch to liquid. Mr. Vincent sat at his desk in the front corner, his nose in a book, ignoring Rick and the other students filling the science classroom.

A long table with a stone black countertop and a sink at one end stretched across the front of the room. The walls of the classroom had been plastered with posters that said things like *Think Like a Proton and Stay Positive* and *I Have to Make Bad Puns about Elements Because All the Good Ones Argon* and one with a dozen roses that said *Science and I Have Good CHEMISTRY.* In the back hung a giant periodic table and in the corner of the room stood an emergency eyewash station.

The moment the bell rang, Mr. Vincent stood and addressed the class from behind the center of the table. He brought their attention to the whiteboard, where he had drawn a stick figure at one end and a simplistic drawing of a house at the other, complete with a chimney and a curl of smoke.

"So, let's imagine Plato is tired after a long day of philosophizing and wants to go home to have dinner and see his wife." Mr. Vincent drew a line between the stick figure and the house.

Kelly raised her hand but didn't wait to be called on. "Plato never had a wife."

"Excuse me?" Mr. Vincent capped his marker.

"Plato never had a wife," Kelly repeated.

"And how do you know this?"

"There's a line about it in a song my dad wrote." Kelly stood and began to sing. "Plato never marrrrrr-ried, he kept all the thoughts he carrrrrr-ried, to his grave where he was burrrrrr-ied, in the ground."

"Thank you. That will be quite enough singing for one day."

Kelly sat down, but only after a bow.

"So here's Plato, going to his home, with no wife in it." Mr. Vincent redrew his marker line. "Though who's making him dinner, I don't know."

"He can make his own dinner," Kelly said, and some of the other girls said things like "he sure can" and "you tell him, girl!"

"I heard that Plato was gay," said a boy in the back row. Several kids snickered.

A kid with a high-pitched voice joined in. "I heard all the ancient Greeks were gay."

"So?" said a kid wearing a T-shirt with a Spider-Man logo on the pocket.

"Yeah, there's nothing wrong with being gay. It's

just how some people are," said a girl with a long braid running down her back.

"This is no talk for the classroom," said Mr. Vincent.

He turned back to the whiteboard, but the girl with the long braid raised her hand and asked, "Wait, what's no talk for the classroom? That Plato was gay, that some kids laughed, or that we said there was nothing wrong with being gay?"

Mr. Vincent looked flummoxed. "None of it. Look, I have a limited amount of hours to teach you a great number of things, and we simply don't have time for this, or any other conversation that is not about science. If you want to talk about these things elsewhere, I encourage you to do so."

"I know just the place!" said the girl with the braid. "Has anyone heard of the Rainbow Spectrum? It's an after-school club for LGBTQIAP+ rights. I know about it because my sister helped start it a couple of years ago, when she was in eighth grade."

Rick wondered what a meeting for gay kids was like and what they did together. Did they talk about how to be gay? Or how they knew if they were gay? And did you have to know whether you were gay or bisexual or whatever to go? Rick didn't even know what all of the letters stood for.

The girl with the braid continued. "The first meeting of the year is on Tuesday after school, and I'm going. Anyone else want to come?"

"Do I?" exclaimed Kelly. "Yes, yes I do, just in case that wasn't clear."

The girl with the braid turned to her and smiled. "Great! I'm Leila, by the way."

"Kelly." They exchanged a firm handshake.

Mr. Vincent huffed. "Now, if everyone's social calendar is firmed up, maybe we can get back to the physics involved in Plato reaching his home."

Mr. Vincent wrote an equation on the board, and Rick copied it into his notebook along with the rest of the class: *WORK = FORCE x DISTANCE.*

The equation made it sound so easy. Work is just putting in some effort and getting somewhere. As if it didn't matter where you were starting from or which direction you were headed.

Rick was still thinking about the Rainbow Spectrum that evening. Sometimes Rick wondered whether he was gay because he had never had a crush on a girl. But he had never had a crush on a boy either, so how could he be gay? If Diane were there, he would have asked her what she thought. Diane was always happy to share her opinion, and more often than not, it wasn't terrible.

Instead, Rick opened his laptop. He typed into the internet search box *how do you know if you're gay?* The results page was filled with quizzes, so Rick clicked on one. He gave up after the first question that asked him to think about the last five people he *liked*. He went back to the search box and typed in *how do you know if you like someone?* More quizzes, which he avoided, and a list that started off by assuming you already knew who it was you thought you liked. It seemed to Rick that if you knew who it was, you already liked them, and you were just trying to figure out how much.

He spun quarters to soothe his mind, but there were no answers in the dancing coins, and eventually, his stomach growled. He headed to the kitchen, where he found two boxes of macaroni and cheese on the counter next to a large green salad, and a pot of water heating on the stove.

Mom said that a watched pot never boils, but Rick knew that wasn't true. If you could be patient, it was entrancing to watch the water heat up. It takes a long time for tiny bubbles to develop at the bottom, but then they start to rise into little bubble columns that multiply and grow faster and bigger, until trails of steam start to waft from the surface, and then suddenly—poof, the water is in a full boil. Today, the bubbles looked like tiny questions building into curiosity columns that tumbled into larger un-knowns until the pot was a rolling mass of boiling unsteadiness.

CHAPTER V

THE KETCHUP KERFUFFLE

Backpack-laden kids gathered outside Jung Middle School for the second Friday of the school year, with windbreakers, hats, and the occasional umbrella to shield them and their backpacks from the drizzle.

"Wanna come over tomorrow and watch

Nohomeworksburg get destroyed?" Jeff asked Rick from under his dripping-wet jacket hood.

"Yeah!" said Rick from under his. "We're at nine hundred ninety thousand citizens." Just ten thousand from a major disaster. "It's all gonna go down."

"Godzilla cometh, Nohomeworksburg! No one will be safe!" Jeff raised a wet fist in the air, and Rick joined him, as they cheered on the upcoming destruction of the town they had spent the summer growing.

The security guard pushed open the school doors, and a wave of wet students flooded in. The hallway smelled faintly of cleaner, but Rick couldn't tell what had been washed. Certainly not the floors, and most of the walls were covered in bulletin boards with posters saying things like *How to Study* and *The Importance of Eating Breakfast*.

Rick and Jeff joined the swell of students on the

stairs, trudging upstream to the daily misery of middle school. Eighth graders had homeroom on the first floor, and seventh graders broke off on the second, but sixth graders had to hike another flight in soggy sneakers and jeans, where they filtered into chilly classrooms that the boiler room in the basement hadn't yet reached for the day, like some kind of administration-sponsored hazing.

Sneaker squeaks and secret whispers echoed up and down the stairwell, drowning out Principal Baker's declarations that "School has begun" and "It is time to quickly and quietly make your way to your homerooms."

Rick filed into room 326, where students crowded in circles around desks. The football fans huddled in one corner talking about last weekend's game, and a group by the window competed to see who could rap the most lyrics from the latest Angie T song.

Rick joined a couple of other kids around Ronnie's desk. Ronnie was an amazing artist, and he could draw a face on just about anything. Kids liked to challenge him to draw anthropomorphic mailboxes and BMWs and, today, a plate of spaghetti. Rick knew it was mostly in the eyes—put a giant pair of surprised eyes on a meatball and suddenly it's like the rest of the face is there too. But Rick also knew that he couldn't draw nearly that well, and he liked watching the characters appear on the page.

The day went along as smoothly as a line from Ronnie's pencil, until Rick ran into Jeff on their way down to the cafeteria, and they both spotted Kelly hanging a sign in the stairwell. Rick saw it a moment before Jeff did, just long enough to realize what would happen without a chance to do anything about it. It was a sign for the Rainbow Spectrum. There were rainbows at the top and bottom of the poster, and big, bold letters that read *All Are Welcome.*

Jeff hit Rick on the shoulder to get his attention. "Whoa, Rick. Check this out. A buncha gay kids are meeting up! Gross!"

"You're the one who's gross," said Kelly, with her hand on her hip.

"Whatever." Jeff snorted. "Let's get out of here, Rick. I'm hungry."

"Yeah," said Kelly. "Get out of here and take your hate with you."

Jeff banged the side of his fist into the metal handrail as he ran down the stairs. Rick followed, and his stomach bounced on every step, so that by the time they reached the lunch line, his insides felt like a ratted knot and the cafeteria's greasy hamburgers and boiled carrots appealed even less than usual.

Jeff surveyed the room and directed Rick to join him across from a pair of kids who wore matching blue baseball caps with a green letter C on them. They were in Jeff's homeroom, and all four of them had sat together for lunch a couple of days the week before. Their names were Mark and Matt, but Rick couldn't be sure who was who. They were both pale-skinned with a couple of freckles and short brown hair that barely stuck out from under their caps, the kind of kids who became friends because they looked so familiar to each other. Mark was taller than Matt, but sitting down, they could have been twins, or at least brothers.

Jeff interrupted whatever they had been talking about and launched right into the story about Kelly and the Spectrum sign.

"And then that lesbo tried to tell me that I was harassing her!"

"Whoa, dude!" said maybe-Matt. "What did you call her?"

"And before you answer that," said maybe-Mark, "you oughta know my aunt's a lesbian."

"And she could kick your butt!" added maybe-Matt. "She does aikido. She's scary!"

"So now you guys are gonna go all gay on me too?" Jeff's voice grew uncomfortably high-pitched as he tried to yell without being so loud that the lunch staff noticed him. "I'll tell ya this: There was a kid in my class in fourth grade, and he was gay, and I punched him in the stomach."

"Yeah." Maybe-Mark snorted. "And we heard he threw up all over you."

"What?" Jeff's eyes bore down on Rick. "Did you tell them?"

"Chill out, dude," said maybe-Matt. "We heard it from this kid in our English class. Wish I had been there to see it. Sounds hilarious."

Jeff stood, picked up his tray, and said to Rick, "C'mon, let's go find another table."

Rick didn't want to get up. He didn't want to follow Jeff. But Matt and Mark had already turned their shoulders to block him from entering their conversation. Rick picked up his tray and joined Jeff at the empty end of a long table. A half dozen kids sat at the other end. They were playing table hockey with a ketchup packet as a puck. One of them was Ronnie from homeroom, the one who drew eyes on donuts and trash cans. Rick didn't recognize the rest. Ronnie gave a quick wave, but the rest of the group ignored them completely.

Jeff speculated out loud about whether maybe-Mark's aunt was too ugly to be straight, and said that only women who wanted to be men knew aikido. Rick knew it didn't work like that, but he also knew that Jeff was already in a bad mood, so he watched the ketchup-hockey game instead.

The kids took turns flicking a ketchup packet back and forth across the table. One kid with a pink-streaked ponytail had an especially deft style of catching the underside of the packet, giving it a little lift that soared it right toward the opposing goal. Another kid with long, dark fingers flicked with such speed that the defender never saw the packet coming. Ronnie didn't have great aim, but he was a good sport about it, and sometimes, when he did hit one in the right direction, the defender was caught off guard and he scored with a shout of surprised glee.

One heated volley sent a packet flying in an arc over the table and landing on the ground ten feet away. That sparked the attention of Mr. Kyle, the vice principal, who meandered through the cafeteria, alternating between chatting with some students and yelling at others.

"I have been to this group every day this week to tell you to cut it out."

Rick stared down at his hamburger as Mr. Kyle lectured the Ketchup Hockey League.

"If I see one more ketchup packet in the air, every single one of you will spend the rest of lunch at my personal table. Is that clear?"

Mr. Kyle's personal table was the one by the entrance, right across from the food line, where he and the cafeteria staff had eyes at all times. Kids at that table were supposed to be silent and read quietly once they were done eating.

A kid with blond-tipped hair said, "But what if it's not one of us?"

"Phillip—and let's start there, since it's still September and I already know your name. That is not a good sign. No one around you is causing a disturbance. The boys at the far end of the table do not appear to even have any ketchup packets. Therefore, if there is another incident of airborne condiments from this part of the cafeteria, all six of you will be dining in silence."

Mr. Kyle swiped the pile of ketchup-hockey pucks and headed off to dump them back into the box by the cashier.

The kids groaned, and Rick heard one of them complain, "Great! I hadn't put any on my burger yet."

Jeff grinned at Rick. "Watch this!" He withdrew a ketchup packet from his pocket as though unsheathing a sword.

"Jeff!" Rick hissed. "What are you doing?"

"Rick, the world is chaos. I'm just helping it along a bit."

"Noooo, don't . . ."

Before Rick could say another word, Jeff had tossed the ketchup packet high into the air. It twirled about and about as it rose and then fell, landing at the far side of the table, sliding, and dropping onto the floor.

If Mr. Kyle hadn't seen the packet in the air, he

certainly noticed the commotion as Ronnie and the pink-ponytailed kid dove down to grab it and knocked their heads into each other. Jeff, who had already been smirking, let out a laugh but dropped his face into a blank stare when Mr. Kyle arrived.

"What did I *just* tell you kids? First, hand over the ketchup." Mr. Kyle held out his hand and waited until the pink-ponytailed kid planted the packet into his palm, still rubbing the top of his head. "Now, all of you, over to my table."

"He's the one who threw it!" Phillip pointed at Jeff.

Mr. Kyle ignored him. "Up. All of you. Bring your things."

"But it's not fair!"

"What's not gonna be fair is if all six of you have to sit at my table next week as well because one of you had to mouth off. Let's go."

Each one of the kids glared at Jeff and Rick as they pulled their things together. Each of their glares stung Rick, but it was Ronnie's that made Rick not want to finish his lunch.

Once the kids were gone and Mr. Kyle was off herding them to the silent table, Jeff let out another laugh.

"What did you do that for?" Rick asked.

"What?" Jeff shrugged. "We didn't get in trouble."

"But those other kids did."

"Oh, lighten up, Rick. You take everything so seriously. Those kids are a bunch of weaklings. Not a single one of them is going to get back at us."

But Rick wasn't so sure. Maybe none of them would beat him up, but they weren't about to be his friends either. And that's when Rick admitted something terrible to himself: Maybe Jeff was a jerk, even if he wasn't being a jerk to Rick.

• • •

It didn't make it any easier that Ronnie came right up to his desk after math class and asked, "Why do you even put up with that kid?" He didn't say which kid. He didn't need to. Rick opened his mouth, but no words came out. Ronnie shook his head. "Never mind. Looks like you don't know either."

Rick couldn't get the question out of his head. Not as he packed his bag, not through his last class of the day, not through the bus ride home or even as he took a shower to try to flush the questions out of his mind. Why *did* he put up with Jeff? Why was he best friends with someone who sometimes made him feel so bad? Ronnie was right—he didn't know.

CHAPTER VI

ON BEST FRIENDS

Rick rode the rickety, crickety Sunrise Apartments elevator up to Grandpa Ray's floor, wondering how thick the cables were and hoping that J. L., who had inspected it last November, had done a good job. When the elevator stopped with a *ca-chunk*, he stepped out carefully and knocked on apartment 4E.

He managed to keep himself from knocking again as Grandpa Ray answered with the speed of an old man who liked to put his slippers on first. But his impatience showed the moment Grandpa Ray opened the door, when he jumped in and asked, "You ready for some more *Rogue Space*?"

"It's good to see you too, Rick!"

"Oh, right. Hi, Grandpa Ray."

"Come on in. Have a seat in the dining room." Grandpa Ray gestured at a small round table with two aluminum chairs. "Let's take a moment to catch up before we delve into the Bzorki action this time. Care for some tea?"

Rick tried not to make a face, either about tea or catching up. "That's okay."

"Or some hot chocolate?"

"Now you're talking!" Rick could wait a few minutes for *Rogue Space* if chocolate was involved.

Grandpa Ray filled the kettle and set it on the

stove. He set out a pair of mugs, dropped a tea bag into one, and dumped a packet of hot cocoa powder into the other. Then he took a seat across from Rick and asked, "So, how are things going? Anything worth sharing?"

Rick shrugged. Friday had been terrible, with Jeff saying those things, and then the whole ketchup scene and getting all those kids in trouble. But he couldn't think about any of it without thinking about the worst part, which was that he wasn't even sure why he and Jeff were best friends anymore.

Grandpa Ray raised his eyebrows. "Well, if you have nothing, I might have to tell you about my week. It involves a daily walk around the block to check in on the squirrels, multiple episodes of old crime shows, and lots of prunes and fiber supplements. Would you like to hear how that's going?"

Mom used to give Rick prunes when he had trouble . . . well . . . going. He didn't want to hear any more about Grandpa Ray's bathroom issues. Even if it meant facing his own problems. "Well, I guess there's something on my mind."

"Fiber supplements." Grandpa Ray grinned. "Works every time. What's up?"

"Well, remember my friend Jeff?"

"Jeff the jerk?"

"Grandpa, that was two years ago!"

"What was?"

"Wait, you don't know about that?"

Grandpa Ray shook his head.

"Then why did you call him a jerk?"

"No offense," said Grandpa Ray, "but any kid who makes fun of another kid for liking *Rogue Space* is kind of a jerk. Tell me this story. Sounds like a good one if you remember it from two years ago."

Rick told Grandpa Ray about the day the fourth-grade crew painted sets for their play of *Charlotte's Web*. "So I was painting some hay bales, and Jeff was working on the sky, and then a kid came by and dropped a piece of wet painted paper on the back of Jeff's shirt."

"Wasn't he wearing a smock?"

"He said it looked too much like a dress."

"Well, *that's* reasonable." Grandpa Ray rolled his eyes.

"And it turns out the paper had been painted on purpose so that it looked like one of Charlotte's spider webs, but with the word *jerk* inside."

Grandpa Ray laughed. "Sounds like that kid knew something you still haven't figured out."

"Grandpa Ray!" It was one thing for Rick to question his friendship with Jeff. It was another for Grandpa Ray to say something.

"Sorry. I shouldn't make fun of your friends." Grandpa Ray's eyes shifted left and then right. "Not even if they're jerks!"

"Anyway." Rick shook his head. "That isn't even the best part of the story. Because once Jeff realized what had happened, he went up to the kid and punched him in the stomach." Rick stopped, not for effect, but because he realized he was talking about Melissa, and that Melissa wasn't a *him*.

"Okay, so he punched the kid," Grandpa Ray encouraged Rick to continue.

Rick chuckled, remembering the scene, and told Grandpa Ray, without names or pronouns, about how Melissa had barfed, and how it had flown through the air in an arc as if in slow motion, and how chunks of food had rolled down Jeff's stomach and landed in a smelly pile at his feet.

"That is disgusting!" cried Grandpa Ray.

"Totally vile!" agreed Rick, still laughing.

"And you're happy this happened to your best friend?"

"Well, he did deserve it."

"So you admit it, your friend is a jerk." Grandpa Ray poured water from the now steaming kettle into the two mugs.

"Only to some people." Rick sounded like he was trying to convince himself as much as Grandpa Ray.

"And that makes it any better?"

"I mean, he's not a jerk to me."

"I'm not impressed." Grandpa Ray narrowed his eyebrows.

"And we have a lot of fun together. Just yesterday, we were playing a video game, and we watched Godzilla destroy our town!"

"And this was fun?"

"Yeah!" Rick grinned, remembering how they had cheered when the beast had appeared out of the ocean and begun eating everything in sight: citizens, cars, buildings, roads, until the population crashed down to one and Godzilla thumped his fists to his chest. "And he waited until I was there to let the monster loose. Thomas would have just played without me and I would have missed it."

"Well, that's something, I guess. So what were you going to tell me about him?" Grandpa Ray placed the mugs on the table and sat back down.

Rick sighed when he thought about the ketchup packet flying through the air. "Never mind. It was another story about him being a jerk, I guess."

"Why am I not surprised?"

"You're lucky." Rick wrapped his fingers around the cup of too-hot-to-drink-yet chocolate.

"How so?"

"You're a grandpa. You don't have to worry about things like best friends."

Grandpa Ray closed his eyes for a moment and covered his mouth with his hand. Rick could feel a cloud of sadness settling around them. When

Grandpa Ray moved his hand, his smile was gone. "You're right. I already lost mine."

Grandma Rose.

Rick took Grandpa Ray's other hand and squeezed it twice. It didn't feel like an old person's hand, the way Grandma Dawn's did, where the veins stuck out and the skin felt like it was tired of holding the muscle and bones inside. Grandpa Ray's hand was thicker and rougher, more like Dad's, and he turned it palm-up to squeeze back.

"I'm sorry. I didn't mean to make you think about her."

"No, it's okay. It's good to think about Rose sometimes." Grandpa Ray took a deep breath and let it out through pursed lips. Then he did it again. "She was a big part of my life for a long time, and in some ways, she still is."

"Does watching *Rogue Space* make you think of her?" asked Rick.

"It sure does."

"Is that a good thing or a bad thing?"

"Most of the time, it's a good thing."

"And the rest of the time?"

"The rest of the time?" Grandpa Ray echoed. "The rest of the time, it's a very good thing. Now let's get to watching the second *Smithfield Special*."

Rick had never thought of Grandma Rose as Grandpa Ray's best friend before. He thought about them watching *Rogue Space* together. They probably sang the theme song and quoted their favorite lines at each other.

Rick couldn't imagine having a best friend he got along with like that, much less losing them.

CHAPTER VII

THE RAINBOW
SPECTRUM

The Rainbow Spectrum signs around school announced that the first meeting would be Tuesday at three o'clock. They also said things like *Your Story Matters* and *A Place to Be Yourself.* Rick wondered whether *being yourself* included having a possibly-a-jerk best friend.

One minute, Rick was pretty sure he was going. The next, he was pretty sure he *wasn't* going. Then he was. Then he wasn't again. Monday turned into Tuesday as the idea of going to the Rainbow Spectrum meeting turned in his mind.

At lunch, after one of the times he decided he was going, Rick told Jeff that he would be checking out the paper-folding club after school. Jeff would tease him for the rest of his life if he knew where Rick was really going, but he wouldn't be there to find out. The moment the required school day ended, a cartoon puff of smoke would be all that was left of Jeff.

Roughly two thousand decision changes later, in last period, Rick was sure he wasn't going. How could he go if he didn't even know why he felt like going? What would he say? Was it enough to say that he'd never felt about a girl the way his best friend did? Was it enough to not know? Rick had already put on his jacket and was in the stairwell between the first and second floors when he saw a Spectrum sign that said *Because you have questions.*

And that's how Rick ended up turning around, climbing back up the flight, and walking toward the classroom with the brightly colored Rainbow Spectrum sign hanging from the doorknob. Closer. Closer. The door was open, but he couldn't see how many kids were inside. He wasn't sure whether it would be worse if it was empty, with just Kelly, Leila from science class, and the faculty adviser staring at him, or full of gay kids and lesbian kids and bisexual kids and transgender kids.

He walked toward the door. And past it. He reached the end of the hallway, took a sip from the water fountain, and was just about to make decision change 2,002 to head down the stairs and out of the school completely when a chubby white kid a bit shorter than him, with a wave of green hair hanging over one eye, rushed by.

"Excuse me," the kid said, and Rick moved out of the way.

Rick took another sip of water, and as he wiped his chin, he told himself, "This is it." His legs drove him toward the door before his brain could disagree. He slipped in right behind two tall kids wearing matching T-shirts that said *Jung Middle School Spring Musical* on the back.

The classroom was bright, and a dozen kids were scattered inside. Mostly, people were gathered in twos and threes, though a few sat alone. Kelly and Melissa were there, of course, in the front row, along with Leila. Today her hair was back in a long ponytail instead of a braid. The three of them were talking to the teacher adviser, who sat in a chair across from them. There was another kid Rick recognized from his Spanish class chatting with the green-haired kid. The spring-musical-shirt kids joined a tall girl who wore a jean jacket covered in patches of the titles of Broadway shows.

Rick took the seat at the end of the third row and watched the clock as more people trickled in. It was 2:55 and the meeting wasn't set to start until 3:00. They were long minutes. Rick looked over the room, wondering who these kids were and whether they had told anyone where they were going, especially the ones who sat alone like he did. The Latinx kid with glasses and a comic book T-shirt. The white kid with a thousand freckles who was biting her nails, a tennis bag slung over the back of her chair. The East Asian kid with long, purple-tipped hair and a hat that looked like a cupcake.

Right at three o'clock, the teacher adviser popped up from his chair. His short sandy hair was only a shade darker than his suntanned skin. He was wearing a lavender shirt, khaki pants, and a purple bow tie.

"Good afternoon, everyone, and welcome to the Rainbow Spectrum. My name is Mr. Sydney, and I'll be your group adviser this semester. As some of the seventh and eighth graders know, Ms. Abrams, who usually runs this group, is on leave this semester. I'm happy to report that she had the baby three weeks ago." He waited for the wave of whoops, whispers, and awwwws to pass. "And that she, her wife, and little Max are all doing wonderfully. Ms. Abrams will be coming back to school in January.

"In the meantime, I am elated, enthralled, and exhilarated to be here. When I was a kid, groups like this were barely starting up at a lot of colleges, much less in middle schools. I can already tell this is going to be an exciting year. Before we do anything else, let's do a go-round, where we all introduce ourselves. In addition to sharing your name, grade, and preferred pronouns, I welcome you to tell us briefly what brought you here today. It's not required, but it would be nice to hear some of your thoughts. Zoe, I believe you were active in the group last year. Will you start us off?"

Zoe was the girl with the patched-up jean jacket. "Hi, I'm Zoe, I'm in eighth grade, and I'm bisexual. My preferred pronouns are *she* and *her*. And I'm here because I think LGBTQIAP+ rights are really important."

"Thank you, Zoe. To be clear, you don't need to tell us your sexual orientation if you don't want to," said Mr. Sydney.

"Oh, but I want to!" said Zoe. "How is someone supposed to ask me out if they don't know I might be interested?"

The two kids wearing the spring musical T-shirts went next—Xavier, who shared that he had been coming to the group since he'd started sixth grade two years ago, and Yaya, who announced that he was "supergaaaaaaay" with a wave of his hand.

"I'm Ellie, lesbian, eighth grade. *She*, please," said the girl with the cupcake hat.

A soft-spoken kid with dark hair and bright red glasses said, "Hi, I'm Mika. And I guess I use *she* and *her*, but I never really thought about it before."

Then it was the kid who had rushed past Rick in the hallway's turn. "Hey, everybody. I'm Green."

"Like the color?" asked Ellie.

"Yep!" Green said with a wide smile. "You've heard of people with red hair being called Red? Well, I'm Green."

"Cool," said Ellie, with a toss of her purple-tipped hair.

"Yeah, so I'm Green, and I'm in sixth grade and enby." Green saw some puzzled looks from around the room and clarified, "*Enby* from *NB*, or *n*onbinary."

Mr. Sydney addressed the class. "Nonbinary refers

to people who do not identify as either male or female. Do I have that right, Green?"

Green nodded.

"And your preferred pronouns?"

"I'd *prefer* not to have pronouns at all," Green said with a shrug.

Yaya joined in. "It *is* kind of messed up that we talk about the pronouns we *prefer*. Like it's our favorite flavor of ice cream or something."

"Right?" said Zoe.

"What if we ask what pronouns a person *uses*?" asked Ellie.

Green nodded. "Okay. Hey, everybody, I'm Green. I'm in sixth grade, and I *use* the pronoun *I*. And I have no idea what you all are supposed to do." Green sounded a bit annoyed, but grinned to show that their annoyance was at pronouns, not at anyone in the room.

A few of the kids turned to Mr. Sydney, who shrugged back.

"You could use the singular *they*," said Yaya.

"What's that?" asked Leila.

"Ooooh! The singular *they*!" Kelly's already naturally musical voice sounded ready to break into song. "I read about that this summer. Like, *They don't want to use either he or she for their pronoun.*"

"I am an English teacher, you know," said Mr. Sydney, frowning.

"I know. And I also know that we already use the singular *they* all the time," said Kelly.

"Maybe you do," said Mr. Sydney. "But my sense of grammar is pretty strong."

"But what if someone really wanted it?" asked Melissa. "Wouldn't you use it for them?"

"Well, I would try, but I would think it would get really complicated," said Mr. Sydney.

"You didn't seem to mind when I did it." Melissa grinned.

"Pardon?"

"I asked whether you would use it for *them*, and you didn't even notice."

"Notice what?"

The room was silent for a moment.

Yaya was the first to say something. "Oh, I get it!"

Green's smile turned into an audible chuckle, and Ellie joined in half a moment later with a long "Ohhhhhhhhh." Soon half the room was either laughing, ohhing, or nodding, while the other half was looking at them with puzzled faces.

"Would someone care to enlighten the rest of us?" asked Mr. Sydney.

Zoe spoke up. "Melissa used the singular *they*. She asked if you would use it for *them*, but she was only talking about one person."

Mr. Sydney's mouth hung open until he shut it

with a snap. He looked at Zoe, and then over at Melissa, who smiled. He closed his eyes for a few moments, and when he opened them, he said, "Fair point. So, Green, what'll it be? Care to navigate unexplored linguistic terrain with me?"

"What?" asked Green.

"I think he means, 'Do you want to use *they*?'" said Kelly.

"Oh, um, sure. I mean, I guess that's better than anything else." Green tossed the long part of their hair out of their eyes and gave a thumbs-up. "Next?"

"I'm Ronnie."

Rick's head shot up from where he had been staring at the ground, listening to all these kids who sounded like they already knew everything about themselves. It was Ronnie, from homeroom and the Cafeteria Ketchup Kerfuffle.

"I'm in sixth grade, and my pronouns are *he* and

his. I'm a straight guy, as far as I can tell, but my moms are queer."

Rick had known Leila and Kelly would be there, and he wasn't surprised to see Melissa. But he hadn't expected Ronnie. It made him worry who else could be hidden behind some other kid. For a moment, he even wondered whether Jeff could be out in the hall, overhearing everything that was being said. Meanwhile, the circle continued around him.

"I'm Leila. I'm in sixth grade and use *she* and *her*, and I don't really know yet, but I've been doing a lot of reading and thinking, and I might be bisexual."

Then it was Melissa's turn. Rick wondered if she would tell everyone. He decided that he wouldn't if it were him.

"Hi. My name is Melissa, and I use *she* and *her*. I'm in sixth grade, I'm Kelly's BFF, and my connection to the community is that I'm a transgender girl."

"Aw, yeah!" said Green. Melissa gave Green a thumbs-up.

"And it's not a secret, but it's also my information to share. So I'm happy for all of you to know, but please don't tell people outside of this room."

"So, uh," asked Mika, "what was your name before?"

"That"—Melissa paused—"is nonov."

"Nonov?"

"Yeah. Nonov your business!"

Melissa shared a high five with Kelly. A few kids chuckled, and the theater kids laughed out loud.

"Good one, Melissa!" said Mika. "Sorry I asked."

Kelly went next. "Hi. I'm Kelly Arden. I'm straight, but I'm a proud ally."

"Not to be harsh," said Zoe, "but ally isn't really an identity to be proud of. And you're new, but we talked about this last year, and we don't use that word as a noun here anymore. Allying is something you do, not someone you are."

"Then what's the *A* for in LGBTQIAP+?" asked Kelly.

"Asexual," said Zoe. A few kids nodded, but others looked confused. "Asexuality is when you don't have any interest in, like, ever doing the deed with anyone."

The word *asexual* buzzed in Rick's head like a fly looking for a place to land as introductions continued around the room. His stomach felt tingly. Not nervous, exactly, but not calm either. More like drinking soda too fast and having the bubbles dance around inside his body. Rick's turn was only two kids away, and then one.

"I'm Sam," said the kid next to Rick. "I'm so glad this group exists. I'm in seventh grade, and my pronouns are *they* and *them*."

That made it Rick's turn. "Hi, I'm Rick, I'm in sixth grade, and I'm a *he*." He might have stopped there, except that everyone was looking at him to continue, which both made Rick feel like he needed to say something and made it harder to talk. "I'm . . . um . . . just here to check things out."

"Welcome, Rick," said Mr. Sydney. "This is a great place to explore."

"Um, thanks."

After introductions had finished and Mr. Sydney had talked a little bit about how the group would be a "safe and affirming space," with the focus of the group driven by student interest, they brainstormed plans for the year.

Some students wanted a place to talk about the problems they were dealing with, especially at home. Others wanted to protest local businesses that didn't support LGBTQIAP+ rights. Pretty much everyone said they wanted a space to be themselves. No one said they wanted a space to figure out who that was. But then again, neither did Rick.

When the meeting was over, Rick slipped out the door while the rest of Spectrum was chatting and gathering their things. He jogged down the hallway, jumping down the last four steps of each flight, and ran down the block, new words buzzing through his head. According to the schedule, the next bus was leaving in three minutes.

There would be another bus in ten minutes, and another ten after that, but Rick was hoping for a quiet ride. Even if none of the kids from Spectrum took his bus, the other after-school clubs were letting out too, and the next bus was sure to be full of kids laughing and pushing each other and knocking into the people who were getting up for their stops with just enough of a *sorry* to not get lectured by some angry-looking old man.

Rick could see the bus pulling over while he was still half a block away, and he waved his hands above his head as he sprinted. He reached the corner, panting, as the last of three women with bright scarves over their gray hair stepped down.

A blast of air-conditioning welcomed Rick in. He swiped his pass and took a single seat halfway back. There were a couple dozen people on the bus, some with shopping bags, and one with a tall cardboard box. Most of them traveled alone and stared at their phones, unaware that they had just missed sharing the bus with a rowdy pack of middle school students.

Rick wished he had a phone, but Mom and Dad said that he wouldn't need one until high school. When he had asked how high school was any different from middle school, Dad had asked whether he would like to wait until college to get a phone, and that was the end of that. If Rick had a phone, he would look up the word *asexual*. He glared at people with their phones, probably playing games and refreshing their social media accounts to find out who just ate a bacon sandwich. They had no idea how much some people actually needed access to information.

At home, Rick was relieved to see that Dad wasn't in the kitchen on a coffee break. Most days, Rick didn't mind chatting with Dad, as long as he didn't mention girls. He was a funny guy, and if he didn't have too much work to do, he would sometimes challenge Rick to a game of checkers. But today, Rick was on a mission. He pulled out his laptop and typed *asexual*.

The screen filled with links to essays, glossaries, and checklists. Asexual meant you weren't sexually attracted to people, or didn't want to do that kind of thing with them. You could want to have a boyfriend or a girlfriend, though. If you were *aromantic*, you weren't romantically attracted to anyone. There were other words too, like *grayromantic* and *graysexual* to describe people who were occasionally attracted to people romantically or sexually, and *demiromantic* and *demisexual* for people who only had those feelings after developing a deep connection. It was a little confusing, but also a relief to see so many possibilities.

Maybe there was a reason Rick didn't know who he *like* liked, and maybe it was that he didn't *like* like anyone. When Jeff, or someone else, said a girl was hot, Rick could sometimes name the reasons they said that—hair and face and bodies and all that. He could guess which boys Diane would say were cute too. But he never would have thought about those people that way if someone else hadn't said it first. And he had had that tingling in his pants grownups talked about, a few times, but it was never about a person. It warmed up something deep in his chest to know that he wasn't the only person who felt that way. Or rather, didn't feel that way.

CHAPTER VIII

OUT OF SYNC

Friday evening, Rick was on his computer, waiting for Mom to arrive home with Diane. He had three tabs open to lists of ways people named how they felt about themselves and other people. He didn't know which of them he was, or if he was any of them at all, but the words were exciting to read. And lots of people online shortened asexual to *ace*, which sounded downright cool.

Rick was still in front of the screen when he heard Mom's car pull up. He shut his laptop and ran into the living room so that he could be sitting there, watching television and looking casual, when Diane came in. Rick couldn't have explained why he wanted to act relaxed for his own sister, but there he was, remote in hand, rapidly flipping for something half-way decent to watch. He settled on a cooking channel. It was a commercial, but whatever was on couldn't be too bad.

The door opened moments later. Diane dropped a large duffel bag by the front door, kicked off her shoes, and was already sitting next to Rick on the couch before Mom was inside.

"You mind?" Diane asked, her hand out. "I haven't

had time to watch a thing at college, and after listening to Mom in the car for the last hour, I just need to chill, you know?"

Diane popped through a dozen channels until she found a show she liked called *Happy Trailers to You* about converting old RVs into surprisingly luxurious homes.

Rick found himself looking more at Diane than at the television. She looked different, but he couldn't say how. Her long straight dark hair was the same, and the way she curled her feet under her legs as she sat on the couch was the same. She was wearing a new university sweatshirt, but that wasn't it. It was like she was shinier somehow, but he didn't think she had started wearing makeup.

"What are you staring at?" asked Diane.

"Nothing."

Diane didn't say anything else until the start of

the next commercial. "So how's life been here on the home front?"

Rick shrugged. "Not too bad. Dad discovered green smoothies last week and has been serving them for breakfast, but he calls them super shakes and doesn't mention the kale."

"Ugh!" said Diane. "Thanks for the warning. My roommate's been making them too. There was a recipe on the internet that went viral or something. What I don't get is why you would ruin a perfectly good drinkable treat by throwing grass and leaves in it. Literally *grass* and *leaves*."

"That sounds like the kind of thing a kindergartner gets in trouble for."

"It sounds like a sin upon fruit smoothies."

They laughed together, then grew silent.

"Diane?" Rick asked quietly.

"Yeah?"

"Can I ask you a question?"

Diane let out a deep sigh and flopped her head in Rick's direction. "If it's anything more complicated than whether secret kale is a good idea, I'd wait until tomorrow."

Rick took the hint and went to his room to twirl Washingtons. Asexuality was definitely more complicated than kale.

Tomorrow came, and with it a thousand near-but-not-quite opportunities for Rick to bring up the topic with Diane. And limitless opportunities to wonder about her reaction. She would probably be surprised but nice. Maybe even too nice—so nice that it was clear she was faking.

Rick worried so long that it was time for the Ramsey family barbecue before he said anything. Mom grilled burgers and Dad made vegetable skewers. Grandpa Ray came over with a big bowl of salad,

Rick made a fruit-and-cheese plate, and Diane baked cookies.

The barbecue wasn't terrible, but Rick wished that he and Grandpa Ray hadn't had to skip a week of *The Smithfield Specials* for it. Diane talked a bunch about college and how great it was to have control over her schedule. Mom and Dad reminisced about their own times in college and how they had met as seniors and Mom had almost failed her last semester classes and how Diane had better never do anything like that. Grandpa Ray was the quiet guy in the corner that Rick barely knew from family events, not the *Rogue Space* lover he had met a couple of weeks ago.

After everyone had eaten their fill and then some, and everyone but Rick and Diane had fallen asleep on the patio, the siblings went inside to watch a couple of episodes of *Extreme Calligraphers' Challenge*.

"I told the people in my dorm not to tell me what

happened," said Diane as she arranged pillows around her on the couch.

"Does anyone else at college watch *ECC*?"

"Turns out, nobody had ever heard of it." Diane shrugged.

The contestants were designing birthday cards. The host, Bastian, would choose his favorite and give it to his boyfriend at the end of the episode.

Rick saw his opening as the commercials started and dipped a toe into the pool of conversation. "So, um, do *you* have a boyfriend?"

Diane chuckled.

"Or, um, a girlfriend?"

Diane kept laughing.

"What?"

"You're adorable when you ask about dating." Diane rustled Rick's hair.

Rick batted Diane's hand away. "Don't call me adorable!"

"Whatever. Do you want to know or not?"

"Yeah."

"Well, I'm kinda hanging out with this one guy, Carlo. He's okay."

"How did you know you liked him?"

"Oh, you know, you get those special feelings: Your skin gets electric, and you both get a little shock when you touch. You'll know when it happens."

Rick felt like he was treading water. "What if I don't like anyone?"

"Not even me?" Diane batted her eyelashes.

"Diane! I mean the special feelings you're talking about. I don't feel like that about anyone."

"Of course you don't!" laughed Diane. "You're too young for dating."

Rick pressed further. "But what if I don't ever get those special feelings?"

"Then, whoever it is, you don't like her." Diane shrugged.

"No, I mean more like, what if I don't get them for girls at all."

"Do you get them for boys?" Diane asked.

"Do you think I'm gay?" asked Rick. Rick didn't think he was gay.

"I have no idea. You haven't told me. Are there any boys you like that way?"

"No."

"Well, then. I guess neither of us knows yet. I wouldn't worry about it. You're just a kid, and besides, boys mature slower than girls."

There was nothing to do but plunge in. "Have you ever heard of someone being asexual?"

"Sure. There's an ace girl on my dorm floor, but you can't be ace."

"Why not?"

"You're too young. Don't worry about it. I'm sure it'll all work out for you soon enough. Enjoy being a kid while you can."

"You sound like a grown-up."

"Whatever. You love me. Now hush so we can see whose birthday cards will get them an RSVP into the final round."

And there they were, back on the surface. Breathing came easily, but the potential of drowning hadn't yet faded from Rick's consciousness. And Diane had thrown a dud of a life preserver.

She went back to school the next afternoon, and their hug was nothing like their parting hug three weeks ago. Both of them squeezed, but not for very long, and not at the same time.

CHAPTER IX

PRONOUNS AND
PURPOSE

Rick took his seat behind Melissa in homeroom on Monday. Once morning announcements were done, Ms. Medina let the class talk quietly, as long as they remained in their seats.

"Hey, Melissa?" Rick could barely even hear his

own words, so he repeated himself, louder and leaning forward.

Melissa turned back. "Hey."

"Could I ask you a question?"

"I guess."

"How did you know that you were a girl?"

Melissa paused, then recited the line she had rehearsed over the summer. "It's not my job to justify myself to you."

"Oh! I didn't mean . . . I'm sorry . . . I didn't mean to . . ." Rick's tongue tripped over itself.

"People don't usually mean to. But I'm a girl because I'm a girl. That's why." Melissa didn't look angry, but she didn't smile either.

"I meant, how did you stick with it, even though everyone kept telling you that you were too young to know?"

Maybe it was the look in Rick's eyes. Or maybe it

was the year that Melissa had spent with a therapist, convincing her mother that she wasn't too young to know who she was. Either way, Melissa didn't turn back around.

"Never mind," Rick said to her. "I don't want to be rude. I just think you're really brave."

"No, it's that"—Melissa scratched at her elbow—"that's not what most people mean when they ask. And really, I don't know. I don't think I'm that brave. It's just who I am, and it was really hard to try to be someone else."

"Oh," said Rick. Sometimes it was really hard to be Rick. Maybe that was because the Rick he was trying to be was someone else.

"Can I ask you a question?"

"It's your turn."

"Why did you come to Spectrum last week?"

Rick froze.

"I mean, whoever you are, that's your business,

120

and that's cool and all. I just thought that you were . . . Well, Kelly thinks you're a homophobe."

"Oh." Her words landed like a stone in Rick's stomach. A homophobe was someone who didn't believe in rights for LGBTQIAP+ people. Diane had called Thomas that when he used the word *gay* as an insult.

Melissa continued. "Mainly she thinks that Jeff is a homophobe and anyone who's willing to hang out with a homophobe is a homophobe too."

"What do you think?" asked Rick.

"I don't know." The bell rang before Melissa said anything else.

"Hey, can I come over after school?" Jeff asked the next day as he tossed the remains of his lunch into the trash and dropped the orange tray onto a stack.

"Yeah," said Rick. "Oh, wait. No."

Tuesday was Rainbow Spectrum day.

"Uh . . . I . . . uh . . . er . . ." Rick's mouth contorted with each nonsense syllable.

"Or are you going to that origami group again?"

Of course. Rick had forgotten about last week's excuse. He heard his mom's voice saying that you need a great memory to tell a good lie.

"You okay?"

"Yeah," said Rick, recovering. "It's just that it's called paper folding. We use a bunch of different techniques."

"You sure you don't want me to come over instead? I got the new *Wheels at Warp Speed* last night, and it's awesome." Jeff pulled the corner of a video game box out of his backpack, revealing the back end of a black car with flames pouring out of the exhaust.

"Maybe tomorrow."

"Sure, maybe." Jeff shrugged.

Meanwhile, Rick felt like he was folding himself into some sort of paper puzzle. Kelly thinking he might be a homophobe was enough to convince him to attend the second Rainbow Spectrum meeting, but Jeff finding out that he was going was enough to make him lie about it.

This time, Rick entered the classroom on the first try. Kelly, Melissa, and Leila were there, as were Green and some kids Rick didn't know. Green waved at Rick. Rick responded with a small, nervous smile, but inwardly he beamed that Green remembered him. Rick took a seat next to a kid with short hair and pale freckles who hadn't been there last week. Other kids filed in after him, including the three tall theater kids: Xavier, Yaya, and Zoe. Ronnie was one of the last to slip into the room.

"Okay, then," said Mr. Sydney, who was wearing a black-and-gray knit vest over a bright pink collared shirt. "Welcome to the Rainbow Spectrum. I'm excited to see so many returning faces, plus some new ones."

He clapped his hands together and held them tight as he spoke. "I've been doing a lot of research, and I want to apologize for my ignorance last week. The singular *they* has a rich history in English, and as I learned on one blog, it is more important to be respectful than to be right. I was caught up in the rules of grammar instead of the function of language. Thank you for educating me, and I hope that you'll keep letting me know when I need to catch up to speed. And I'm going to do my best so that you won't have to."

Rick couldn't remember ever having heard a teacher apologize about not knowing something before. From the looks of pleasant surprise around the room, neither had anyone else.

"To start today, I'd like to switch up one thing about our introductions, based on something I read. This time, let's make stating your pronouns optional, no matter what they are—*he, she, they, ze,* or something else."

Green looked relieved.

"You are welcome and encouraged to share, especially because that can make it easier for others to open up, and your answer can change, but I don't want anyone to feel they have to give an answer every week if they're thinking it over. So let's do our go-round. And for an icebreaker this week, tell us a word you love."

Mr. Sydney wrote down people's words on the board as they went around the room:

LOVE

FRIENDSHIP

JELLY BEANS

FABULOUS

HABERDASHERY

MARIPOSA

PANSEXUAL

PALIMPSEST

POTATO

MINUET

FIERCE

OOZE

ANTIDISESTABLISHMENTARIANISM

TRUST

SUNDAY

VIOLET

FREEDOM

MAYBE

DAFFODIL

NAPTIME

Rick's word was *Sunday*. Until last month, he would have said Saturday, since sometimes he played video games with Jeff and he never had school the next day, but now that Sundays were Grandpa Ray days, it had won out.

Mr. Sydney was the last to introduce himself. "My pronoun is *he*, and my favorite word is a new one for me this week." Next to the list of words, he wrote in giant capital letters: *QUILTBAG*.

"Well, it starts with a *Q*, like queer, so I like it," said Green.

"Good eye!" said Mr. Sydney as he wrote the word *queer* running down vertically, starting with the *Q* from *QUILTBAG*. "I came out at a time when we mostly talked about our community as *gay* or *gay and lesbian*." He wrote the words using the starting *G* and *L* on the board. "And I genuinely appreciate the inclusivity of LGBTQIAP+, but it was a little unwieldy on my tongue. So I did some sleuthing and found this gem that a feminist artist named Sadie Lee came up with. Any ideas what the other letters stand for?"

"Bisexual!"

"Transgender!"

"Intersex!"

The words flew at Mr. Sydney, and he wrote them down as fast as he could.

"Asexual!"

Rick didn't call it out loud, but in his mind, he added *and aromantic.*

"That just leaves the *U*," said Kelly, "and I'm *unsure* what that means." Kelly chuckled at her own joke, but Mr. Sydney wrote it in.

"You are exactly right, Kelly," he said. "Many, many people, especially your age, are unsure, and that's valid."

"Ohhhhhh," said Kelly, mirroring Rick's thought. "That's good."

"QUILTBAG," said Yaya. "I like it. It's super sayable."

"Way easier than LGBTQIAP+," Xavier agreed.

"It's not *that* much easier," said Zoe.

"One of my moms makes quilts," said Ronnie, "and I really like that word, because quilts are made up of all these different little bits. And each one of them is just a weird thing on their own—"

"Who are you calling a weird thing?" said Green.

"No, I mean—" Ronnie shook his head.

"Just kidding," said Green. "I'm pretty weird. But you're right. Each of the pieces of the quilt is unique, but it's when they come together that things get really good."

"But what about *P*, for pansexual?" said Leila, an eyebrow raised.

"Oh, right!" said Yaya.

"We can keep using the plus sign to say we know that we can't ever cover it all," said Ellie. She wore the same cupcake hat from last week, but now the tips of her hair were dyed blue. "Does that help?"

Mr. Sydney added a big plus sign to the end of the word.

"I guess," said Leila. "But I still like LGBTQIAP+ better."

"Me too," said Zoe. "No offense, but QUILTBAG sounds kind of funny to me."

"Fair points," said Mr. Sydney. "I didn't mean to

say you *need* to use this acronym. I was just offering an alternative."

"Well, I'm going to use it! I'm a total QUILTBAG+!" said Green. They did a little dance in their chair, complete with jazz hands.

"I like it too," said Yaya, "but I don't want to make anyone feel bad. Is there anyone who doesn't like it so much that no one here should use it?"

The room was quiet.

"Leila?" Mr. Sydney prompted.

"I'm okay, as long as people use the plus sign and I don't have to use it if I don't want to."

"That," said Mr. Sydney, "sounds like a community-based compromise if I've ever heard one." He added LGBTQIAP+ to the board.

"So, what are we doing today, Mr. Sydney?" Green asked.

"I was thinking that we could spend the meeting

talking a bit about what we want to do this year as an organization."

Zoe's hand was up immediately. "I think we need to have better books in the library. I mean, look at us, we're the Rainbow Spectrum and we're still learning a lot of this stuff."

"Yeah," said Xavier. "And some kids might not have friends they can talk to about being QUILTBAG+, so if they could find some good books in the library, it could really help them."

"That's very thoughtful of you," said Mr. Sydney. "But books cost money."

"We could have a fundraiser," said Ellie.

"We were saying at the end of last year that we wanted to get more involved in educating the whole school on queer issues," said Yaya.

"So let's get educating!" said Zoe. "All in favor of raising money to get new books with queer content into the school library, raise your hand." So many kids raised their hands that they didn't even bother counting them. Rick kept his hand down. He thought that having better books in the library was a great idea, but that a fundraiser sounded like more posters, and that sounded like more comments from Jeff.

"That settles it," said Zoe. "We're having a fund-raiser. Or should I say, a *fun*-draiser. Now we just need to think of something *fun* to help us *draise* money for some books!"

People threw out ideas, and Ellie wrote them on the whiteboard.

"A bake sale!"

"A car wash!"

"A fundraiser night at Pizza Pete's."

"C'mon, people," said Ronnie. "Groups do stuff like that all the time. We're the Rainbow Spectrum. We've got to do something exciting, something that makes people think it's cool to be LGBTQIAP+."

"A play!" shouted Xavier.

"A musical!" added Zoe.

"Broadway style!" Yaya stretched his hands out at his sides and shook them with flair. "There's a rich history of queers in theater."

"Do you have any idea how much costumes and sets cost?" asked Kelly. "It would eat up whatever money we make."

"Besides," said Ellie, "the arts department already does a school musical in the spring. Ronnie's right. We gotta be original."

"I've got it!" yelled Green. "Let's do a talent show. It's onstage—"

Xavier, Yaya, and Zoe cheered.

"—but there are no sets," Green finished.

"And no scripts to memorize!" added Leila.

"We can all just do the thing that's right for us," said Green.

"We can call it a cabaret!" said Yaya.

"Anyone here got a talent?" asked Ellie.

More than half the kids raised their hands.

"Awesome!" said Kelly. "I'll pass around a sheet. If you want to be in the cabaret, put down your name and what you want to do onstage!"

"Let's not get ahead of ourselves here," said Mr. Sydney. "We have to make sure the auditorium is available . . ."

"I'm sure there's a time that'll work," Kelly said as she ripped a page out of her notebook and wrote RAINBOW SPECTRUM CABARET across the top. "The longest journey begins with a single step."

"What?" asked Leila.

"Oh," said Melissa. "That's just Kelly turning into her dad. He says stuff like that all the time."

The conversation turned to ridiculous parents and the indignities suffered by their children while Mr. Sydney tried to steer the conversation back to fundraisers. The talent show sign-up sheet made its way around the room.

"What if we're not sure what we want to do yet?" asked Chris when the sign-up sheet reached him.

"That's okay," said Kelly. "Just put down your name and we'll worry about it later."

"What about kids who aren't here?" asked Green.

"We can add more names next week," said Ellie.

When the list reached Rick, there were already a dozen names on it. Singing was the most common option, and a few kids were going to play musical instruments. The theater kids were going to do some theater thing together, and Devon was going to dance. But there was also Dini with a magic act and Green juggling and Chris writing in that he would *probably read a poem or something.*

Rick wondered whether *spinning quarters* counted as a talent. He thought about what it would be like to be onstage, showing off. The thought was light and airy for a moment . . . but then it dropped with a thud.

Jeff. Not that Jeff would be there. But Jung Middle School wasn't that big, and word traveled fast when sixth-grade reputations were on the line. Rick passed the paper along without signing up. When the meeting ended, he bolted out the door and to the bus stop.

He reached the corner just as the bus did. He took a seat and checked down the block before the bus pulled away. Sure enough, half a dozen kids were meandering toward the bus stop, and worse, one of them was Ronnie. Rick lowered himself in his seat until only his hair was visible through the window. He didn't breathe until the bus pulled away.

CHAPTER X

SECRETS SHARED

"You know what I've had a hankering for lately?" Grandpa Ray asked when Rick showed up for their weekly visit. "A big old bowl of popcorn! Sound good?"

"Sounds great!" said Rick, looking over at the kitchen nook. "But where's your microwave?"

"Don't have one. Rose always used to say she'd

leave the gamma waves and the infrared lasers to science fiction, thank you very much. So we never got one. And after she passed, well, it seemed silly by that point."

"But then, how are you going to make popcorn?"

"The same way I always have. And the way everyone did, back before people started nuking their food."

Grandpa Ray set a large aluminum pot on the stove, poured in a stream of thick yellow oil, and swirled the pot by its handles to spread the liquid across the bottom. He dropped in three kernels and turned the heat on high.

"How's school been, grandkid o' mine? Anything interesting?"

"Not much," said Rick. "Homework, mostly."

"Sounds like school to me."

The words *not much* popped around in Rick's head like Senator Smithfield and her crew flying through space. Like the Bzorki, they couldn't find a place to settle because they didn't fit anywhere. What part of school was *not much*? Jeff getting kids in trouble over airborne condiments? Going to the Rainbow Spectrum? Learning the word *asexual*? Not to mention trying to remember which teachers had which rules about how to turn in homework and whether they freaked out if you whispered to your neighbor for a pen.

Grandpa Ray melted butter in a small pan. After a minute, Rick heard a kernel pop. The second and third soon followed. Grandpa Ray turned off the flame under the butter, poured a large handful of popcorn into the pot, put the lid back on, and gave it a few shakes. The kernels started exploding soon afterward, with a metallic clink as they bounced off the lid. The trickle grew to a flood, as if each kernel landing sparked two more to pop.

Every few seconds, Grandpa Ray would give the pot a shake that released a puff of steam and the smell of fresh popcorn, until the pops slowed and then ceased, like the last few kids dashing into the classroom when the bell rang. Grandpa Ray lifted the lid to reveal a batch of popcorn that perfectly reached the brim of the pot.

"Wow!" said Rick. "I've never seen popcorn made like that before!"

"The world is a wonderland of adventures," said Grandpa Ray, pouring the fluffy nuggets into a large, wide bowl. "Here, taste one."

Rick took a large handful and stuffed it into his mouth. They were bland, and chewing them was like gnawing on Styrofoam.

Grandpa Ray laughed. "I said taste *one*. We haven't put salt or butter on them yet. Go get yourself something to drink."

Rick opened the fridge to find some lemon seltzers and a six-pack of blackberry soda. He took one of the sodas and drank a third of it in one gulp.

Grandpa Ray took the melted butter from the stove and poured it over the popcorn. Then he salted it generously, tossed it around, and offered the bowl back to Rick.

Rick picked up a single kernel and eyed it suspiciously. He placed it carefully between his front teeth and crunched. "Not bad." He picked up a small handful and tossed them into his mouth. "Pretty good, even."

"My pleasure. *Rogue Space*?"

"*Rogue Space!*"

Rick and Grandpa Ray sat on the couch, munching away, as Senator Smithfield, a Citruvian refugee of Garantulan raids, rose through the Bzorki ranks to become the only non-Bzorki member of the Legion of Truth.

Neither of them said another word until the credits rolled over a Garantulan night sky and Grandpa Ray turned to Rick. "So, what's this secret you're holding?"

"What makes you think I have a secret?"

"Kiddo, there is not a thing about you right now that doesn't just scream, *I have a secret.* Now, spill."

This was the point of no return. From here, he could lie and say some other thing. Something, anything, other than *the* thing. But the way that Grandpa Ray looked at him—not expecting honesty, but hoping for it—Rick opened his mouth. And nothing came out.

"Or if you don't want to talk about it, that's okay too." Grandpa Ray shrugged, but his voice dropped with disappointment.

"No, it's not that. I want to talk about it a lot. It's just . . ." Rick felt a dozen sentences aiming for his mouth tangle into a traffic jam mess.

"Take a deep breath," Grandpa Ray advised.

Rick did, and held it before releasing it, the way his dad did.

"And another."

Once the words stopped chasing each other, Rick tried again. "You know how guys are always talking about how hot girls are?"

"Some guys, anyway."

"Well, I don't like to. I don't even think it. I don't want to do the things with girls that most guys talk about. And I don't want to do that stuff with guys either. Like, I don't think I even really want to kiss anyone."

"I see." Grandpa Ray twirled a tuft of his white hair around his finger.

"And then I learned the words *asexual* and *aromantic*."

"Ahhhh." Grandpa Ray nodded slowly. "Sounds like what you're describing."

"That's what I thought. I'm not sure which one I am yet, though."

"And that's okay." Grandpa Ray gave a sharp nod of approval. "I'm glad you told me, and I hope you'll keep sharing as you know more. And, Rick?"

"Yeah?"

"I'd love you however you are. Even if you were a Garantula."

"Grandpa Ray, if I were a Garantula, I don't think even *I* would love me."

Grandpa Ray laughed, and Rick did too. Being a Garantula was pretty awful, even to other Garantulans.

"So you believe me?" asked Rick.

"Of course I believe you. You are the person who knows yourself better than anyone else. There are lots of different ways of being. Lots of different kinds of people, and lots of different kinds of relationships."

"Maybe," said Rick, and the room grew silent, like there was still more important conversation to have. "But what if it changes and I like girls at some point? Or boys?"

"Then it changes and you like girls at some point. Or boys. Or both. Or other people too."

"Dad says I'm a late bloomer."

"Maybe. Or maybe you're blooming now, and you're just not the kind of flower he was expecting."

Grandpa Ray's eyes stared at nothing in particular. Rick tried to figure out what he was focusing on, but he couldn't see anything special. It was as if Grandpa Ray was looking at something, or someone, from twenty years ago. He opened his mouth, but instead of saying anything, he closed his lips. He did that again, and then a third time.

"Are you okay?" Rick asked.

"Yeah, I'm fine." Grandpa Ray paused. "But if we're sharing, I should probably tell you something about me. I know you never met your Grandma Rose, but she was fabulous. Simply remarkable. She loved *Rogue Space* even more than I did. And we had this secret thing we did, where we would dress up like some of our favorite characters and go out together."

"Like in public?"

"Yep," Grandpa Ray said, his voice quiet. "We would go as a Bzork/Garantula couple to conventions, and it would freak people out when we would kiss right in the middle of the exhibit hall."

"I'd be freaked out to see a Bzork and a Garantula kissing too. But I'm not really sure that counts as a secret."

"Well, there's more. It's something I haven't talked about in a long time, and something I haven't talked about with anyone since Rose left us."

"Why me?"

"Because I'm not getting any younger, and not telling anyone isn't doing me any good."

"Wait, are you sick?" Rick jumped up. "Are you dying?!"

Grandpa Ray laughed. "Not yet! And hopefully

not for a good long while. But I am sick of keeping a secret."

"Oh, phew." Rick sat back down. He had never seen an adult quite so nervous to say something before, especially not to a kid. He put his hand on Grandpa Ray's knee and patted it a few times. Grandpa Ray put his hand on top of Rick's and rested it there. Rick could feel Grandpa Ray's bony knee through his pants.

"Your Grandma Rose used to make the most beautiful Bzork."

"You were the Garantula!" cried Rick.

"Not only that," said Grandpa Ray. "I was a Garantulan woman."

"Ohh." Rick tried to act calm, but the inside of his head was screaming.

"Quite the detail about your old grandpa, huh?" Grandpa Ray smiled, mostly with his eyes.

"Are you still my grandpa?"

"What are you talking about?"

"Are you saying you want to be a woman? Or, I mean, you are a woman?" Rick added, remembering what he had learned from Melissa and Spectrum about *wanting* to be something versus *being* it.

Grandpa Ray shook his head. "Oh no, not at all."

"Wait. If you're not a woman, then what are you?"

"Well, you could call me a crossdresser, but really, I'm the same Grandpa Ray I've always been. Just like you're the same Rick you've always been. We know a little more about each other now. That's all. And just like I wouldn't tell anyone about you without your permission, I hope you won't tell anyone about me."

"Of course not," said Rick. Then he asked, "Does Dad know?"

"No."

"Thomas? Diane?"

Grandpa Ray shook his head.

"Well," said Rick, "thanks for telling me."

Grandpa Ray ran his finger along the bottom of the empty popcorn bowl and dabbed the salt onto his tongue. Rick did the same. It was the perfect ending to a conversation that was meaningful but not exactly sweet.

"So, how was your visit?" Dad asked Rick on the way home.

"It was okay."

"That good, huh?"

"It was fun."

"More *Rogue Space*?"

"Yup, and Grandpa Ray made popcorn. Right on the stove."

"He's been saying that he's been having a craving lately. Did he drizzle melted butter on top?"

"He did! It was delicious."

"I'm sure it was."

The car was quiet for a bit after that, but the question in Rick's head got louder and louder, until he had no choice but to release it. "What was it like growing up with Grandpa Ray and Grandma Rose?"

"Oh, you know, what's it like growing up with any parents? What's it like growing up with me and your mom?"

"No, I mean, is Grandpa Ray now like he was then?"

"Well, he's got a lot less hair now, and the hair he's got is a lot more white." Dad chuckled.

Rick didn't care about Grandpa Ray's hair. "Did you watch *Rogue Space* together when you were growing up?"

"*Rogue Space* didn't even hit the air until I was in high school," said Dad, "and by that time, I was too busy going on dates to stay home and watch a television show with my parents. Besides, it was your Grandma Rose who was really into the sci-fi and all that. I think he got hooked on the show because of her. He was deeply in love with her."

After they pulled up in front of the house and Dad turned off the ignition, he turned to Rick. "My dad and I are different people. Real different. But he's a good man. And you're a good kid, bud. I'm glad you two are getting along so well."

"Me too," said Rick, thinking Dad had no idea how much. It sounded silly in his head, but Grandpa Ray felt like family in a way that Rick had never noticed before and couldn't explain. Dad, Mom, Diane, Thomas—they were all part of his family, of course. But Grandpa Ray? He felt like the pillow on the couch at home that said *Family is where you store your heart.*

CHAPTER XI

LESS BRAVE THAN
A POSTER

"Oh, look! It's one of the new signs for that gay group!" Jeff pointed at a Rainbow Spectrum poster on the way down to lunch. "They're gonna have a *cabaret.*" Jeff said it like he was making fun of a fancy French cheese.

Rick had known that Jeff would find out about

Cabaret Night, but he hadn't realized it would happen so quickly.

"Probably a bunch of freaks dressing up like girls."

"I don't think it's just that," said Rick, his voice barely a whisper. He thought about Ronnie and Green and Ellie and Xavier and Zoe and . . . okay, Yaya said he wanted to dress up like the pop star Miss Kris for the grand finale, but that didn't make him a freak.

"Cover me," said Jeff, pulling a marker out of his bag.

Rick wasn't sure how to do that, much less whether he wanted to, but in the jostle heading downstairs, no one really noticed two kids stopped on the mid-flight landing. Jeff worked quickly, and within seconds, he was done.

"Check it out!" Jeff beamed.

"Oh. Wow." Rick stared at the sign. Leila had designed it, and Kelly had probably hung it. And Jeff had totally destroyed it with a dirty doodle.

"C'mon." Jeff tugged at Rick's shirt sleeve. "Let's get out of here."

They made their way downstairs.

"Just play it cool," said Jeff as they entered the cafeteria.

Rick knew Jeff's prime rule for mischief: Never talk about the incident before other people did, because it made you a prime suspect.

Rick was happy not to talk about it. But the defaced sign stuck in the back of his mind. It floated around him through the rest of the afternoon, bounced up and down with him on the bus home, and tucked in with him when he went to bed.

Could he get in trouble for not telling anyone about something Jeff did? And worse than getting in trouble, was it wrong? And if he had done something wrong in not telling someone when it first happened, did the amount of wrong grow the longer he didn't say anything, or was it just the same amount of wrong that he started with?

Being Jeff's friend was a challenge. Some challenges were good. They made you stronger, braver, better. But maybe Jeff was the other kind of challenge, the kind that made you do things you thought you'd never do, like the Donner Party, who got stuck in the Sierra Nevada Mountains and had to eat each other to survive.

When the bell to end the regular school day rang, Rick made his way to Spectrum. He wondered whether anyone had seen what Jeff had done. Anyone other than Rick, that is.

The room was crowded, with more students filing in behind him. Mr. Sydney sent students to pull in chairs from the next room and even then, a bunch of kids sat on tables and a few plunked down on the floor.

After their name and pronoun-optional go-round, Mr. Sydney addressed the group. "Good afternoon, everyone. I'm glad to see so many new people here today, especially given the circumstances."

"Why? What happened?" asked Sam.

"Didn't you hear?" said Leila. "Some jerk went and messed up our poster in the cafeteria. I had to take it down."

Rick's breath stopped. The poster Jeff messed up had been in a stairwell.

"I thought it was the one by room 215," said Yaya.

How many posters had Jeff ruined?

"Rude!" proclaimed Ronnie.

"Not just rude," said Zoe. "This is downright dangerous. It might seem like a small thing, but this is the sign that there are serious haters at this school."

"Well, at least one, anyway," said Green. "They could all have been done by the same person."

"Yeah," said Leila. "But all those times? Someone

must have seen them do it. Someone might have even been playing lookout. That makes them an accomplice."

Rick felt himself sliding down, trying to melt into the chair.

"I don't want to be at the kind of school where people think they can do stuff like that," said a kid who hadn't been to Spectrum before.

"I'll bet it was one of the kids from Handel Elementary," said another with a bunch of thin bracelets on his right wrist. "Those kids are so backward."

"Hey!" said Kelly. "Melissa and I went to Handel."

"So did I," said the kid with the bracelets, "and I got teased for doing ballet until I got to Jung."

"It's because so many of us are Baptiste kids," said Ellie. "We had a whole mindfulness program that was actually kind of cool."

"Kindness inward, kindness outward," said Zoe, putting her thumb in the air and wiggling it around.

Half the class copied her movement, whispering, "Kiko, kiko, kiko."

"It's a thing we learned at Baptiste," Xavier explained to the sixth graders who hadn't gone there. The seventh and eighth graders from other schools had seen it before, and some of them had even started to join in when they noticed kids doing it.

"Yeah, well, it works," said Zoe. "No one at Baptiste ever got pushed or shoved or yelled at because anyone thought they were gay. We even had a trans kid come out in third grade. I'll bet there are more now."

"I remember that kid," said Xavier. "We were in fifth grade then. That means he must be in, like, sixth grade by now."

Green cleared their throat and gave a little wave.

"Oh!" said Zoe. "But I thought that kid was a—"

Green cleared their throat again, louder this time. "Yup, that was me. And yeah, there were a couple of trans kids when I left. I was the only enby, though."

Sam raised their hand slowly.

"Okay," said Green, "the only one who was out at the time. But I don't know if I would have been out in third grade if I was at Handel. Some of those kids are brutal."

"You went to Handel, right, Rick?" asked Ellie.

"Uh, yeah." Rick studied the tile pattern on the floor.

"Was it really as bad as all that?"

Rick shrugged.

"Well, I mean, there's a range of kids anywhere, right?" Xavier said. "And we don't even know that the kid who did it went there. Maybe they went to London Elementary, or maybe they moved in from out of town. Or maybe they were even a Baptiste kid."

"Everybody knows all the worst kids come from Handel," said Ronnie.

"We're not Slytherins," said Yaya. "I went to Handel."

"Yeah," said Xavier, "and you were kind of a jerk when I met you."

"Ouch," said Yaya, fanning himself with a spread hand.

"Handel has its problems, sure," Melissa agreed. "But there were some cool people there."

Kelly tipped her hand in a grandiose bow from her seat.

"I was thinking about Principal Maldonado," said Melissa, and Kelly threw the back of her hand against her forehead in a false show of outrage.

"Maybe we could write a letter to him and recommend he start using Kiko," said Ronnie.

"Who?" asked Kelly.

"The principal at Handel."

"Principal Maldonado is a *she*," Kelly said.

Ronnie winced. "Oops. Don't tell my moms I did that."

"I think it's a great idea," Leila said.

"Maybe we could form a committee," said Ellie. "Who here wants to work on a letter to Handel Elementary School?" Ellie, Leila, and three other kids raised their hands.

"Well, I think it's more important than ever that we have the cabaret," said Kelly, "both to raise money for books for the library and to show everybody that we're not afraid. Anyone who wants to work with me on planning, join me over here." Kelly headed off to the cluster of tables on one side of the room and a bunch of kids joined her.

The rest of the group decided to make new posters to hang to advertise the cabaret. They drew curtains and spotlights and wrote things like *LOVE IS INFINITE* and *THE RAINBOW SPECTRUM IS UNAFRAID.*

Rick joined them. But he *was* afraid. Afraid that someone would realize that he was trying to be someone he wasn't. And he wasn't sure whether he was more afraid of being found out by Jeff or by the kids at Spectrum.

He jogged for the bus after the meeting let out, but the bus was still two blocks away when he reached the corner. He could already hear the voices of kids behind him.

Rick considered walking around the block and waiting for the next bus, or the one after that, if he had to. And he might have, if the first kid to reach the stop hadn't been Ronnie.

But it was, and he said, "I think I know who did it."

Rick looked ahead and said nothing.

"Don't you?"

Rick looked down at his shoes.

"Don't worry. I don't think it was you."

Rick concentrated on the crack in the sidewalk, tracing it up and down with his eyes, the cement drifting apart, coming together, drifting apart again.

"Why do you still hang out with him, anyway? He's like an egg salad sandwich that's been out in the sun too long."

The bus pulled to the curb with a loud hiss. Ronnie took a seat with the kids from Spectrum. Rick sat in a single seat, too far away to hear what they were saying but close enough to hear their laughter.

CHAPTER XII

A STELLAR IDEA

Rick was glad it was the weekend. The weekend meant two days without worrying about whether Jeff was going to destroy the new Rainbow Spectrum posters. Even better, it meant watching the last of *The Smithfield Specials* with Grandpa Ray.

He didn't know what they would do together once the specials were over. They could keep watching *Rogue Space*, but Rick had seen the new ones and even Grandpa Ray admitted that most of the old ones were hokey. Besides, Dad had hinted that he should try to get Grandpa Ray out and about. Diane used to go swimming with him, and before that, he and Thomas used to bird-watch. But Rick hated the way beach sand felt between his toes, and the most he could say about birds was *That's a blue one, and I think maybe it's kinda biggish.* There had to be a place they could go that would be fun for both of them.

That's when Rick had a wonderful idea. He went online. Serendipitously, he found what he was looking for, and better yet, it was the following weekend. Rick printed out the information and folded the paper six times, until it was a thick little square he could stuff into his jeans pocket.

. . .

The elevator rattled up the four flights to Grandpa Ray's front door.

"Hey, Rick!" Grandpa Ray greeted him with a hug. "Good to see you."

"You too!" Rick thought about the paper in his pocket, but he didn't mention it yet. He wasn't sure what Grandpa Ray would think. So he settled into his regular seat and tried to ignore the lump pressing against his thigh.

"How was your week at school?"

Rick sat, his mouth open, his breath caught behind his tongue. He had been trying hard all weekend not to think about school, because whenever he did, all he could think about was Jeff defacing the posters.

"That good or that bad?" asked Grandpa Ray.

"It was horrible. Just horrible. Remember my friend Jeff?"

"The kid who hates *Rogue Space*." Grandpa Ray sneered.

"It's just that, well, Jeff is a huge jerk." It was a relief to say it, like the idea had been clogging up his throat and finally dispersed. Some of it he exhaled, and the rest coursed through his body, forcing him to feel the truth. "I hate that my best friend is a jerk."

"What did he do now?"

Rick told Grandpa Ray about Jeff's poster attack.

"And you were there when he did this?"

"One of the times," said Rick.

"And what did you do?"

"Nothing." Rick felt a tear forming in the corner of his eye. He hadn't done anything, anything at all.

"Sounds like it's time for a new best friend," said Grandpa Ray.

The words hung in the air, as though their truth kept them from fading.

"You're right," said Rick. "But how did I not know that until just now?"

"Sometimes it's hard to see the worst in our friends, because it reminds us of the worst in ourselves."

"Oof." The sound came involuntarily, from deep in Rick's stomach.

"I know. And the only way out is through."

Rick bent over until his head reached his knees, and he sobbed, Grandpa Ray rubbing his back with his firm, steady hand. He cried until his shoulders shook, and then he went limp.

When Rick sat up, he saw a pair of wet streaks running down Grandpa Ray's face too. They faced each other, small smiles growing until there were a pair of wide grins on their faces. Then Grandpa Ray bared his teeth, which made Rick giggle.

Grandpa Ray handed Rick a tissue, then blew his own nose as well. For a moment, Rick wondered why Grandpa Ray had cried. Then he remembered Grandma Rose, and that reminded him of the paper in his pocket.

"I had an idea for what we can do next weekend, now that *The Smithfield Specials* are done."

"Oh?" Grandpa Ray raised a thick eyebrow.

Rick pulled out the wad, unfolded it, and smoothed out the grid lines so that the page lay nearly flat. Then he handed it to Grandpa Ray. It was covered in spaceships and aliens, and read, *SPACE CON is coming to Kiely Arena with special guest, Amy Salazar of* Rogue Space!

"Oh." Grandpa Ray's eyes shone for a moment. Then a wave of sadness passed over his face, taking his smile with it. "I don't know, Rick. It wouldn't be the same as . . . as before."

"I know," said Rick. "Grandma Rose wouldn't be there."

Grandpa Ray's cheeks blew up, and he let the air

slide out of his mouth with a *whoooosh*. "I wish I could say that was the only problem. I just can't imagine going in everyday clothes."

"Why would you go in everyday clothes? Isn't the whole point of going to a con that you get to dress up?"

Grandpa Ray tilted his head to stare at Rick from the corner of his eye. "Wait . . . are you suggesting we . . . ?"

"Grandpa Ray. You're gonna need to get a little better with words if you plan to talk to anyone at Space Con. Yes, I want to go with you. And yes, I want you to dress up however you want. Even if that means dressing up as a woman. Especially if it means dressing up as a woman! But maybe not as a Garantula."

Grandpa Ray's face wavered between a giant grin and a goofy grimace as he realized what Rick was saying.

"I was thinking maybe you could go as Senator Smithfield! And I could be a Bzork. I want antennae!"

Grandpa Ray blinked a few times, let a few joyful tears drip down his face, and read the flyer again. Then his smile returned. "Wow, this is next Sunday! I only have a week to plan my costume!"

CHAPTER XIII

UP IN FLAMES

In homeroom the next day, Ronnie waved at Rick to come over and see the bicycle he was sketching. He had drawn huge eyes on the front, using the handlebar as a kind of mouth. It looked both excited and a bit nervous. Rick could relate.

Melissa joined them, and when she did, Ronnie

complimented her on the new signs for Cabaret Night with a look of exaggerated innocence in Rick's direction. A chill trickled from Rick's neck down the length of his spine and out to his shoulders.

"Thanks. A whole bunch of us made them. Kelly and I just hung them up."

"Well, you did a really good job," said Ronnie. "They're everywhere."

The word *everywhere* landed like a lump in Rick's chest, and he was relieved when the bell rang and they had to head to their seats. All morning, he kept his eye out for the Cabaret signs, and every time he saw one, the tension in his shoulders dropped when he saw that it had been unaltered, especially when he found the one in the stairwell that he had made himself.

By lunch, Rick had started to relax.

Rick and Jeff were eating alone at the end of a long table of kids talking about graphic novels when Jeff raised his thumb. Mr. Kyle released Jeff to use the boys' room and he muttered, "Follow me."

"Why?" Rick asked, but Jeff just shrugged and kept walking. With a sigh, Rick lifted his thumb in the air.

The bathroom was empty, but someone had been there earlier, because they had taped a sign for the Rainbow Spectrum cabaret to the door on the inside.

The words *Rainbow Spectrum Cabaret* were in bold cursive, and a spotlight shone on a shadow figure. Underneath that, the poster said, *Be Who You Are!* and in smaller print, *Tickets $1–20—give what you can. All proceeds will be used to purchase LGBTQIAP+ titles for the Jung Middle School library!!* followed by the date and time of the show. At the bottom was a note that read, *If you see anyone messing with this sign, please report it. Ally with us to fight hatred.*

Jeff pointed at that part and laughed. "Good thing you're the only one here, Rick."

"Why's that?"

"Check it out!" Jeff pulled a red lighter out of his pocket.

"You brought a lighter to school?!"

"Took it from Gene. I'll put it back when I get home. He'll never know it was gone. Besides, he'd appreciate what I'm about to do."

Jeff tore the sign from the door, taking a piece of tape with it and ripping the top right corner.

"Wait, what are you about to do?" Rick heard his voice shake.

"What do you think? I'm gonna set this sign ablaze!"

"You can't do that!"

"Watch me!"

But Rick was done watching. His arm shot out, knocking the lighter out of Jeff's hand. It skittered under the sink. Rick tried to grab the paper out of Jeff's other hand, but Jeff was already diving for the lighter.

"What is wrong with you?" Jeff yelled once he was standing again, with the lighter in one hand and the now rumpled poster in the other. The poster for the group of kids Rick was starting to think of as his friends. A group of kids who never deserved to be talked about the way Jeff did.

It didn't matter anymore that Jeff would restart his video games so Rick could play. It didn't matter that they laughed together until they had forgotten what they were laughing about. And it certainly didn't matter that they had once been closer than brothers. Rick didn't want to be friends with someone who was so mean.

He shook his head back and forth a few times before he said it. "Jeff, I don't want to be your friend anymore."

"Oh, you don't mean that," said Jeff.

"I do." Rick brushed away a tear before it could fall.

"What?! You're gonna call off our friendship over some stupid poster about some gay kids?" Jeff's face was turning red. "You can't do that! We're best friends!"

"Not anymore." Rick let the next tear fall. It didn't matter anymore what Jeff thought of him.

"Are you *crying* now? You're such a baby! You know what?" Jeff's lips quivered with anger. "I've carried you long enough. You were nobody when I met you, and you're nobody now."

"I'd rather be nobody than somebody awful."

"You think I'm awful?"

If Rick didn't say it now, he might not ever say it. "Yeah. Yeah, Jeff. I think you're awful. You're mean to a lot of kids, and you talk about girls like they're food on a menu. You make fun of *Rogue Space*, and when I wanted to try out for the play in fourth grade, you told me only idiots would want to do that." Once Rick started, the words flowed out, and he watched Jeff shrink in front of him. "You didn't just mess up that one Rainbow Spectrum sign. You're the one who ruined all of them. And now you're trying to do it again!"

Jeff shoved his chin forward. "Let me guess, you're one of them."

With the walls of friendship crumbling, it simply didn't matter anymore what Jeff knew. Or thought. Or thought he knew.

"Yeah, I've been going to Spectrum."

"*Yeah, I've been going to Spectrum,*" Jeff mimicked. "You've been hanging out with those freaks. What, are you gay or something?"

"Something." Rick stood upright, feeling the wet streak on his cheek grow cold.

"What the hell is that supposed to mean?"

"I'm questioning." Rick heard his voice echoing back at him, ringing as true as it was nervous.

"You mean, you don't even know what you are?"

"I may not know who I am. But I'm sure about what you are."

"And what am I?" Jeff stared down at Rick.

"You're a homophobe and a bully. And I'm through with you."

"Yeah, well, I've just got one thing left for you." Jeff held the paper far out in front of himself, held the lighter to the edge of the page, and tossed the sign out of his hand, preparing for an all-consuming flame.

Instead, the paper fluttered to the ground with a wisp of smoke, a fringe of ash along the bottom, and a thin orange glow already burning itself out.

Rick snorted. Then he turned around, his heart beating so loud he was sure Jeff could hear it, and walked deliberately out of the bathroom and to the empty end of a table in the corner of the cafeteria. Trying not to listen to Jeff call him a *freak* and an *idiot*. Trying not to cry. Failing on both counts.

• • •

Rick sat there, his head buried under his arms, for the rest of the lunch period. He didn't know where Jeff had gone, but he didn't care, so long as it wasn't near him. He didn't get up when the bell rang. He didn't even realize that someone had taken the seat across from him until they spoke.

"So now what?"

Rick looked up to see Ronnie, his eyebrow and the corner of his mouth raised in hopeful inquiry. He dumped Rick's backpack on the table. "You're welcome, by the way."

"Thanks."

"I saw you two get up." Ronnie's voice was quiet. "It didn't look like anything good was going to happen next."

"It didn't."

"He's the one who destroyed the posters, isn't he?"

Rick nodded. "I guess I have to tell Principal Baker."

"You're gonna rat on your friend?"

"He's not my friend. Not anymore."

"Congratulations."

"That's kind of a weird thing to congratulate me for."

Ronnie laughed, then stopped short. "Do you want me to come with you? To the principal's office, I mean."

"You'd do that?"

"Yeah. *Plus* I'd love to get out of the beginning of English."

With an awkward pair of grins, they headed down to the office, checked in with the school secretary, and two minutes after the bell to start the next period rang, they were in Principal Baker's office.

Ronnie didn't do any of the talking, but he nodded and, just when Rick thought he was going to bail, squeezed Rick's hand. The story came falling out of Rick's mouth, from the first time Jeff commented on the signs, to his marker defacings, to the burnt paper that was probably still on the floor of the bathroom. Principal Baker thanked them for their time and recommended that they get to their next class as quickly as possible.

"You coming to Spectrum tomorrow?" asked Ronnie, once they were in the hallway.

"Isn't it the cabaret rehearsal?"

"Is that a problem?"

"No. I just didn't think I was a part of that."

"And I didn't think you would ever drop that deadweight of a friend. Come to the meeting tomorrow. It's time you made some new friends."

Science was half done by the time Rick got to class, and before his head had recovered from his meeting with Principal Baker, he was back in the halls, navigating his way to Spanish. If he had been thinking clearly, he would have taken the second-floor hallway to avoid the office, where Jeff was inside, surely fuming. But if he hadn't had reason to avoid Jeff, his brain wouldn't have been so muddled in the first place.

As it was, Rick did pass by the main entrance, and in a misfortune of timing, he saw Jeff's mom, Stacey. And worse than that, she wasn't coming into the school. She was leaving, and Jeff was with her.

"Hey, Rick," she said, her voice surprisingly pleasant for a mom who had been called in to school to pick up her kid during the day.

"Hey," Rick said, trying not to feel Jeff's steely eyes boring into his skull.

"Did you hear what this one did?" Stacey lifted Jeff's hand, clasped in hers.

"Yeah, I guess," said Rick.

"He's the traitor who told on me," said Jeff.

"You could learn a thing or two from your friend, Jeffrey," said Stacey. "I don't see his mom getting called in to talk with the principal and a *police officer* about her son starting a *fire* at school."

"That freak isn't my friend anymore," Jeff muttered.

Stacey shrugged. "Your loss." She winked at Rick.

"I hope you have fun with your new friends," Jeff said with a sneer before Stacey dragged him off.

"Thanks, I think I will," said Rick.

CHAPTER XIV

THEATER THRIVES ON SPONTANEITY

The next day's Spectrum rehearsal meeting was held in the auditorium. A giant piece of paper stuck to the wall listed the cabaret program order and who was in the crew. Kids gathered around it, gabbing about who was performing when. Others were gathered around Ellie, the stage manager, asking a thousand questions. Rick stood by the door, watching the excitement.

"You made it!" said Ronnie, giving Rick a high five.

"Yeah, well, this pretty awesome guy told me I needed to make some new friends, so here I am." Rick shrugged, but his delight showed in his smile.

"Do you have a talent?" Ronnie asked.

"What?"

"It's a talent show. Do you have a talent? If you don't, we could use another stagehand, but it would be cool if you had a talent."

"Well . . ." Rick could see quarters spinning in his mind and could smell their oily metal. Then he spotted Kelly glaring at him from across the room. "Never mind."

"What is it?"

"It's nothing."

"Rick, if we're gonna be friends, you've got to

share how you're feeeling. Otherwise, I'll never know you."

"Oh."

"Good one, huh? My moms say that to each other. Except they don't just say friends. They call each other partners in love and life." Ronnie shook his head as if to get the words out of his mind. "So, what's your talent?"

"It's nothing big. But I spin quarters, and I can get five going at once, maybe six. Plus I've been working on a new coin trick where I stop the coin spinning with my finger and it stays standing up."

"Oh! I saw you doing that in homeroom. It looked really cool. You have to do it!"

"Umm . . ."

"That is, if you want to."

Rick pictured himself onstage. He hadn't tried out for the fourth-grade play because Jeff would have made fun of him for doing it.

Then Rick remembered that he was done with Jeff and he was never going back, not even if Jeff begged him to.

"I do," said Rick, surprising himself more than Ronnie. "I really do."

Ellie called the group together into a large circle. "Okay. We only have today to rehearse, so we're not going to see everyone's talents. Instead, we're going to focus on transitions. Getting on and off the stage, Melissa's emcee notes, that sort of thing. We'll go through Yaya's finale once or twice, since this is the only time most of us will get to practice with him, and then we'll take it from there. Any questions?"

"Yeah," said Ronnie. "Is it too late to add one more act? It's short, I promise."

"Theater thrives on spontaneity." Ellie affected a posh British accent.

"What?" said Ronnie.

Ellie dropped the accent. "It's fine."

"Well, Rick here spins quarters!"

"Spins quarters?" Kelly sounded dubious. "What kind of talent is that?"

"It's super cool!" said Melissa. "I've seen him do it! He even tried to show me once, and I was terrible at it."

"Rick, can you show us?" asked Ellie. "Anybody got a quarter?"

Rick took a handful of quarters out of his backpack and made them into a small stack on the edge of the stage.

"He comes prepared!" exclaimed Yaya.

Rick set the first quarter going. The second coin skittered right off the stage, but Rick didn't worry about it. He set four more spinning in a row, the first one still finishing its dance as he set the last one loose.

"Wow!" said Green.

"That's really cool," said Sam. Others nodded and agreed as well.

"I told you!" said Melissa.

Kelly shrugged. "Yeah, I guess that's a talent."

"So," said Ronnie, "is it too late to add him to the show?"

"What do you think, Spectrum?" asked Ellie.

The cheer was as brief as it was sudden, but it was unmistakable. And it echoed in Rick's mind. He'd never been cheered for before, and it made him want to cheer right back. "Hurray for the Rainbow Spectrum!" he called out.

"Hurray for the Rainbow Spectrum!" the group responded.

"I appreciate your enthusiasm," said Mr. Sydney. "And that was quite impressive, Rick. But today needs to be the last day for sign-ups."

"Yeah," said Sam. "We need to design and print the programs."

"If there are no other dramatic reveals, we need to get moving. Ronnie, get Melissa situated and let's run through this thing." Ellie took a black marker and drew an arrow between two acts in the second half and added in Rick's name. "That's better anyway, to break up the two couples singing."

"We're not a couple," said Seeley.

"Yeah," said Trish. "We just wanted to sing together."

"Okay, but try to tell me Mika and Talia aren't going out."

Mika blushed and Talia giggled. Then they raised their already interlocked hands as one.

"I wish we had time to see everyone's acts," said Xavier.

"We will, next Tuesday," said Mika. "There's no reason we need to stay backstage the whole time, is there?"

"We can reserve the front row for performers," said Talia.

"Well, some of us will have fabulous outfits we'll want to do a big reveal for."

"Yaya, you can head back into the dressing room to prepare for the finale."

"And I'll be videoing the whole thing," said Mason, with a thumbs-up to Yaya.

"Great," said Ellie. "I'm glad we've worked out all the details. Now, can we get moving, people? Time is flying."

And with that, Melissa read the introduction to the audience and introduced Xavier, Yaya, and Zoe onstage. They would start off the show with a performance of "Willkommen," the opening number from the Broadway musical *Cabaret*. From there, the performers took turns being announced by Melissa and heading onstage, only to turn right back around and get off again.

Melissa didn't have a piece in the script for Rick, but her ad-lib was just as good as any of the introductions Sam and Tracey had written. "And now

Rick will set your heads spinning with his coin tricks!"

"That was perfect," said Ellie. "More of that, Melissa, and next Tuesday is going to be phenomenal!"

There was only Mika and Talia to bring onstage after Rick, and then it was time to practice the grand finale. Yaya had gotten into his Miss Kris outfit: an electric-blue dress, silky white wig, and two-inch chunky silver heels.

"You look amazing, Yaya!" said Green.

"Totally like Miss Kris!" said Mika.

"I'd let you 'Rock My Heart' any day," Devon said, referencing Miss Kris's latest hit.

"Thank you, thank you!" Yaya said with Miss Kris's lilt. "It'll be even more fabulous next week with makeup." He invited everyone who wanted to dance in the finale to line up. Most of the kids joined, as did Mr. Sydney and his boyfriend, Minh, who had come to help out.

"Do you wanna?" Ronnie asked Rick.

"I don't know. Do you?"

"Maybe, but I asked you first."

And that's when Rick realized that Ronnie wasn't asking whether Rick thought the dance was cool. He was asking whether it looked like fun to Rick, and once Rick understood the question, he knew the answer as well.

"I sure do! You coming?"

Rick and Ronnie hoisted themselves onstage, ignoring the steps at either side. Yaya showed them the dance, which was pretty simple: step to the left-left-right-right-left-left-forward-back. Clap-clap-clap-clap. Throw your hands up and shake with joy. Jump right and do it again.

Once everyone had it down, Xavier and Zoe joined in front, ready with a more complicated routine.

Yaya started the music and joined in. He began the song at the back of the stage and meandered through the crowd during the first verse with a dark cloth draped around him. Right before the start of the first chorus, he landed at the front of the stage, pulled off the cloth, and broke into a dance. It started simply, like the one everyone else was doing, then turned into Xavier and Zoe's steps, and then branched into a dance all his own, moving in ways Rick hadn't known were possible for a person with bones. Everyone cheered when the dance was through.

"Great job, everyone. We are going to make so much money for the book fund!" said Ellie. "No regular meeting next Tuesday. Instead, be here at four thirty to help set up, if you can. Doors to the auditorium will open at five forty-five, and the show will start at six. Invite your friends and family!"

Rick looked around for Ronnie, thinking they

might walk to the bus together. But in scanning the room, he missed who was right next to him.

"Hey there."

Rick jumped twice in surprise. Once because there was someone so close, and a second time because it was not Ronnie but Melissa.

"Oh, um, hi."

"That was really cool what you did with those coins there."

"Thanks." Rick hunted for something to say. "Do you, uh, still play checkers?"

"I haven't played checkers in years," said Melissa.

"Oh." Rick's shoulders dropped.

"I've moved on to chess. Maybe I could teach you how to play."

Rick looked up, not expecting Melissa's smile. "That would be cool."

That's when Kelly approached from behind and

looped her arm through Melissa's. "Melissa doesn't want to talk to you."

"Actually," said Melissa, disentangling her arm from Kelly's, "I do."

"But it's my job as your best friend to protect you."

Melissa lowered her chin so that she was staring at Kelly from under a deeply furrowed brow.

"What?"

"No, Kelly," said Melissa. "No, it's not."

"Your choice." Kelly raised her hands and backed away.

"Sometimes even really good friends can be difficult. How did you deal with that Jeff kid for so long before firing him?" Melissa winked.

"Wait, what? How did—?"

"How did I know?" asked Melissa. "Let's just say good news travels fast. Glad to have you with us, no matter what some people think." Melissa tossed her head Kelly's way. "Chess. Someday soon."

"You got it," said Rick.

Rick found Ronnie and they walked to the bus stop, along with Green, Leila, and Sam, all of them singing "We Are All Beautiful" together, stepping to the left and right and clapping down the block.

CHAPTER XV

GAMMA RAY GOES TO
SPACE CON

Rick had had a soda-fizz feeling in his stomach all morning and he couldn't quite place why. He was going to Space Con with Grandpa Ray, which was exciting, but it felt like something more than that. He packed his Bzorki ears and cape in his backpack as his stomach fizzled.

Rick rode the rackety, crackety elevator up and knocked on the door with a *tap-TAP, tap-TAP, tap-TAP*, like the opening of the *Rogue Space* theme song.

Grandpa Ray answered the door like it was any other day, in his slippers, gray sweatpants, and white T-shirt.

"Oh," said Rick, the sound of disappointment out of his mouth before he was aware of feeling it.

"Oh?" Grandpa Ray echoed.

"I just thought that you might already be in costume."

"You're not," Grandpa Ray countered.

"Well, no. But I thought you'd, you know, be excited about it."

"I'm over the moon!" Grandpa Ray said in an airy kind of way, an uncontrolled grin filling his face.

"So why aren't you ready?"

"I guess I didn't want to disturb you." Grandpa Ray dropped his grin and shrugged.

"Huh?"

"Well, you've never seen me . . . dressed up before."

And that's when Rick realized that the soda-fizz feeling in his stomach was excitement. "And now I have to wait even longer!"

Grandpa Ray laughed. "In that case, I'll be back in a few minutes. I've got everything laid out. You get ready too."

Rick put on his cape and ears, and then he flipped through television channels until he landed on a show about how things are made. The episode was about aluminum foil. The shiny liquid-metal river captivated Rick, and once it cooled into a brick, he enjoyed watching the metal pressed out over and over, until it was flexible enough to be rolled up. Then it was rolled out thinner and thinner, until it was like metal paper.

The final product was being rolled onto a cardboard tube when Grandpa Ray emerged from the bathroom. He wore a long black dress with a thick red sash over his shoulder, a red wig back in a bun, and lots of large silver jewelry, like Senator Smithfield wore when she addressed the Pristine Council.

He looked perfect to Rick. It was as if Senator Smithfield were really there, but with Grandpa Ray's beaming face. The Citruvian temple ridges he had drawn on with makeup looked just like they did on the show, and he had even replicated the scar on his right cheek that Senator Smithfield had gotten as a girl.

Rick realized he had been staring, and worse, his mouth was open. He closed it and tried to think of something to say. "You look amazing! Better than amazing! You look like Senator Smithfield!"

"Why thank you!" Grandpa Ray gave a quick spin. "It does feel pretty great to put on the old garb. And thank goodness this wig held up all these years. I had to dig pretty deep in the closet this morning to find her."

"It's just like on the show!"

"Passed by a lot of memories on the way." Grandpa Ray nodded slowly.

"I'm sorry," said Rick.

"Don't be. First off, it's not your fault. But more importantly, some of the memories were sad, yeah, but most of them were fantastic. Your Grandma Rose was pretty special."

"So are you."

Grandpa Ray dabbed a tear away. "Okay, no more mushy stuff. I'll ruin my face. Speaking of which, have a seat and I'll give you a few Bzorki touches."

Rick wasn't sure what Grandpa Ray meant until he pulled out a metal box that unfolded into layers of makeup.

"Wow," said Rick. "You sure have a lot of that stuff."

"Well, I haven't gone out in a while," said Grandpa Ray, "but I still like to put on a look from time to time."

Grandpa Ray loaded up the soundtrack from last season's *Rogue Space* and plugged his phone into a cylindrical speaker, humming along as he applied a range of colors to Rick's face. Rick didn't have much basis for comparison, but Grandpa Ray seemed like an expert. He acted like one of the people who put on makeup in commercials. When he was done, he held up a hand mirror. "What do you think?"

Rick looked like a Bzork, right down to the cheek lines. He grinned, and the lines stretched out wide.

"Wow! Grandpa Ray, you're really good at this." Rick admired himself in the mirror. "And look at you. If I didn't know you, I would wonder if you were Aida Benson!" Aida Benson was the actor who played Senator Smithfield.

"Why, that's quite the compliment. But I want to make one thing clear to you. No matter how I look, I want you to know that I'm always your Grandpa Ray."

"I know that," said Rick.

"Well, some people who wear skirts and makeup are women. Me, I'm a guy, no matter how I'm dressed. This is a costume, like yours."

"Cool," said Rick. "There's one thing, though."

"What's that?"

"I know you're still my Grandpa Ray, but it might look a little funny if I call you that at Space Con."

"Good point. When I went out with Rose, she just called me Ray and it wasn't an issue."

"What if I called you Grandma Ray?" Grandpa Ray wasn't his grandma, but Rick couldn't imagine calling his grandpa only by his first name.

Grandpa Ray's face went firm and the lightness of his smile was gone. "You absolutely may *not* call me Grandma Ray. I won't have it!"

"I'm sorry!" Rick hadn't meant to say anything wrong.

"I won't have it," Grandpa Ray repeated as a sly

grin trickled across his face. "Not when *Gamma* Ray is sitting right there as a possibility!"

"Gamma Ray!" Rick didn't know whether to give Grandpa Ray a high five or a hug, so he did both.

They had a wonderful time at Space Con, wandering among the booths and admiring people's costumes. They got to hear some of the current *Rogue Space* writers talk about the history of the show, and Rick even got an autograph from the actors who played VerDurZal, the three-headed sage of Kendor Prime. But Rick's favorite part was watching Gamma Ray fill up every inch of his body and share himself with the world.

Driving home, Grandpa Ray asked, "So, how are things going with that friend of yours?"

"Who, Jeff?"

"Who else?"

"He's not my friend anymore."

"Oh really?"

"Yeah."

"What happened?"

Without even closing his eyes, Rick could see the Spectrum sign and the thin line of orange ember where the paper had burned. He told the story. The whole story, including going to Principal Baker with Ronnie. Jeff hadn't shown up for school the next day, and later Rick had heard that Jeff had been suspended for a week.

"Well, sounds like a win-win for you," Grandpa Ray observed.

"Huh?"

"Not only did you get rid of a terrible friend, but it sounds like you're making a new one."

He wondered if Ronnie would be his friend. Maybe Green too, and some of the other kids in Spectrum. Maybe even Melissa.

After the car grew quiet, Grandpa Ray turned on an oldies rock station and hummed along with songs that Rick recognized but didn't know the names of, with crashing cymbals and winding guitar solos. Neither of them spoke again until the end of the trip. Instead, they both dove deep in the caverns of their minds with distant smiles on their faces.

"Good time today, huh?" Grandpa Ray said as he pulled into the garage below his building and eased into his parking spot.

"Super good. And don't worry, I won't tell Dad about . . . you know." He gestured at Grandpa Ray's outfit. "The Smithfield Special."

"Smithfield Special. I like that. I mean, it's not that I want it to be a secret, really. It's just, he's so hard to talk to."

"Don't I know it!"

"But maybe it's time I said something. Once you

break through, he's a pretty good guy. I mean, Rose and I raised him, after all. And times are changing. More people are talking about bending gender roles than they used to."

Dad texted Grandpa Ray that he was pulling up to the curb, so Rick hugged Grandpa Ray goodbye and exited into the bright afternoon air.

"Nice ears," Dad greeted him when he got into the car. It sounded like Dad was being sarcastic, but Rick thanked him with a smile and didn't take them off.

"Did you have a good time with Grandpa Ray?" Dad asked.

"Totally!" said Rick.

"I'm glad to hear it. I worry about my dad sometimes. Especially since your grandma died. Sometimes it seemed like she was the only person who really understood him. I'm glad you're getting along with him. He seems to like you even better than Thomas and Diane. Me, I've never quite been able to connect. Sometimes it's like I barely know him." Dad turned to Rick with a distant thought in his mind, but if he had words for it, he didn't share them. Then he chuckled. "Oh, but look at you."

"What?" asked Rick.

"You've got some lipstick on your cheek!"

Rick pulled down the visor and noted the reddish-purple splotch. He had gotten a kiss from Grandpa Ray. "Oh! Oh, that?"

"Did you meet a pretty girl at the con?"

"NO!" Rick shook his head. "I mean, no. It's just from, um, there was someone there, and they wanted to say hi. But it's not like that."

"It's okay, bud," said Dad. "You're allowed to think about girls."

Rick could have let the moment pass. A month ago, he would have let the moment pass. But a month ago, he had never been to a Rainbow Spectrum meeting and he had a jerk for a best friend.

"I'm really not thinking about girls like that."

"Okay." Dad opened his mouth a few times, but he didn't say anything else.

"I'm not thinking about boys like that either."

"Okay," Dad said again. "Don't worry, it'll happen soon enough."

"I'm not worried," said Rick. "Have you ever heard of being asexual? Or aromantic?"

"I can take a guess what it means. But you're too young to be something like that."

"I'm almost twelve."

"Everyone has their own path."

"And right now, my path is that I'm not interested in anyone."

"That might change."

"It might. It also might not. Either way, it feels

good to have a name for what I'm feeling. Or, um, not feeling."

Rick thought Dad would say something in response, but he didn't, until the silence grew wider and wider, and out of the chasm grew a thought in Rick's mind.

"Dad," said Rick.

"Yeah?"

"Have you ever told Grandpa Ray that you feel like you don't know him?"

Dad gave his head a sudden shake, and then another one, slower this time. "Why, I don't know that I ever have."

"Maybe you should," said Rick.

"Yeah," said Dad, nodding slowly. "Maybe I should."

CHAPTER XVI

Ronnie popped his head into the classroom-turned-dressing-room across the hall from the auditorium. He was wearing all black like a proper stagehand and had to yell over the commotion of sixteen kids practicing a dozen different acts one last time. Green juggled. Mika and Talia practiced their dance moves.

Delia played her violin solo once more. It was too loud to concentrate on quarter spinning, but Rick fingered the quarters in his pockets. He had chosen ten of the shiniest he could find in his jar that morning.

"Are we ready to open the doors?" asked Ronnie.

"Almost!" yelled Xavier as he added a few final touches of blush to Melissa's face. She wore a navy-blue dress with silver polka dots and a wide, silver belt. Xavier popped a silver sequined top hat onto her head and declared her done. She headed out toward the auditorium.

Outside the classroom, the hallway walls were covered in artwork, from Kelly's photographs and Ronnie's smiling sketches to a giant papier-mâché rainbow that Sam and Tracey had made and hung above the auditorium entrance. The hallway itself was filled with people: parents, grandparents, teachers, families with kids, groups of classmates, and tons of noise.

Mr. Sydney sat with his boyfriend, Minh, taking money and stamping hands so people could go in once the auditorium doors opened. Kelly and Leila meandered through the crowd with long chains of raffle tickets wrapped around their necks like necklaces. The tickets were a dollar each, and the winner would get to keep half of the money that was raised. The other half would go to the fund for getting more QUILTBAG+ books into the school library.

"Salutations! Salutations!" Melissa cried as she squeezed through the mass of quieting people to reach the auditorium entrance. "Welcome to you all, and thank you for coming to the Rainbow Spectrum's first-ever cabaret! I'm Melissa, and I'll be your emcee for the evening. Come on in and have a seat. The show will begin shortly!"

She opened the doors and welcomed people with a wave and a smile and a tip of her sequined top hat as they entered. She greeted everyone cordially, except one woman, who she nearly leapt on with a giant embrace and kiss on the cheek.

"I'm so excited to see you onstage again, Melissa!" said the woman. "And this time, I'm ready!" She was dressed in jeans and a simple black long-sleeve shirt, and she wore a pin that said *Support Trans Kids*.

"I love you, Mom," said Melissa. "And take pictures!"

"I will!"

"You're gonna be great, kiddo!" Kelly's father was right behind Melissa's mom.

After another hug, Melissa's mom went with Kelly's dad to find seats near the front.

Rick looked around and found Mom, Dad, and

Grandpa Ray waiting on the line to get in. They each gave him a giant hug, and Grandpa Ray told him to *break a leg.*

Fifteen minutes later, Melissa was onstage and the acts began. Xavier, Yaya, and Zoe went first, because they had insisted that a Broadway opening number was sure to get the audience geared up for the rest of the show. Next was Green, who juggled two oranges and an apple and even took a bite out of the apple while the oranges were in the air.

After intermission was the raffle drawing, which Mr. Vincent won with a hoot they could hear in the dressing room. Roberto started up the second act by playing acoustic guitar. Chris read a poem he had written after that, followed by Mika and Talia, who were good singers with even better dance moves. And then it was Rick's turn.

"This next act is a lot smaller, but don't let that fool you," Melissa announced as Ronnie, Brinley, and Kadyn rolled up the gym mats behind her and replaced them with a table. Meanwhile a screen came down from above. "This kid really knows how to twirl some heads! And some tails too! Because Rick is going to share with us the wonders of quarter spinning! Here's Rick!"

Rick came up to applause and dropped a stack of quarters onto a corner of the table. He looked down, trying to forget that there was an audience of people staring at him and Mason's zoomed-in video on the screen above, where his hands were bigger than his real head. He told himself he was at the kitchen counter at home.

He neatened the stack and placed the first coin between the middle finger of his right hand and the thumb of his left. With a quick flick, he set the quarter spinning and the audience leaned in to watch.

He set a second coin going. The third coin shot forward, right off the table, and in his speed and nervousness, Rick spun the fourth too hard and it knocked the second one out of place. Only one coin remained upright, and it wasn't long before that coin had fallen too.

The audience gave a collective "Awwwwwww!"

Rick shared a look with Melissa and tried again. He took a deep breath, and on the exhale, he set the first coin spinning. Quickly, he fired off a second and then a third. He took another breath before the fourth, and set it spinning perfectly in place. The first coin was starting to wobble but he launched a fifth before it had stopped buzzing. The audience clapped and Rick took a bow.

Melissa shuffled over to Rick while the audience was still clapping. "You still want to do the other part?"

Rick rubbed a quarter between the thumb and

index fingers of both of his hands. He could say no. He could give up. He had already messed up onstage once. He could go for good enough and not chance another mistake. Or he could move forward, into the unknown.

"Yeah," Rick whispered back. "I've been practicing."

"You got this!" Melissa gave Rick a thumbs-up and went back to the mic.

"Amazing, right? Don't let them tell you kids aren't good with money! And now, for Rick's grand finale. I've seen him do it in homeroom, and I promise you folks, this one's gonna leave you on the *edge* of your seat!"

Rick took a quarter in each of his hands and balanced them between the backs of his thumbs and the pads of his middle fingers. A quarter didn't spin nearly as long if you only spun it with one hand, but for this trick, Rick didn't need them to spin for more than a moment. Simultaneously, he spun the coins, let them twist, and then touched the edges lightly enough with his fingertips that he could stop them in midair. Then he let go, and the coins remained, balanced on their sides, until the audience broke into applause that shook the air enough to knock the quarters down.

Seeley and Trish came up after that and sang the 1960s song "My Girl" together, dressed in pastel dresses with long, wide skirts. Xavier had put their hair up in what he called bouffants, which Rick learned was a fancy hair way of saying round and puffy. They left the stage holding hands.

Then the Rainbow Cabaret ended with Yaya and the rest singing and dancing to Miss Kris's "We Are All Beautiful." Rick did the steps and hand claps he'd learned the week before, and thought about the QUILTBAG+ people in his life. Melissa. Green. Himself. He thought about Grandpa Ray dressed as Senator Smithfield. And he thought about real friends, people like Ronnie, who were excited to find out more about him. He thought about everyone onstage, and everyone in the audience. And the more people he thought of, the harder he smiled, until his vision got distorted and his cheeks hurt. But he didn't stop. He didn't want to stop. He smiled and laughed his way through the finale, and when the song was over, he clapped and cheered and shared high fives with the people around him.

Everyone onstage held hands and took a bow, and then they clapped some more. Rick waved at Mom, Dad, and Grandpa Ray in the audience. He even noticed a little kid waving a quarter back and forth with a giant grin on their face.

After the performance, everyone poured into the dressing room to get back into their regular clothes. Rick didn't need to change, but he wanted to be in the air of excitement. People kept congratulating him and a few people offered hugs. Rick wasn't used to having friends who wanted to hug, much less who asked first, and he accepted every one happily, but none so happily as Ronnie's.

"That was really awesome! Maybe we could hang out after school tomorrow."

"That'd be cool," said Rick.

And they did. And the next day at lunch. And the day after that. And the day after that. And the day after that.

Rainbow Spectrum Cabaret Program

Xavier, Yaya, and Zoe perform "Willkommen" from
Cabaret

Green juggles apples and oranges

Devon dances modern ballet to "For Everyone" by J. S. N.
Reynolds

Dini performs magic as The Great Who: Dini

Delia plays Minuet by Boccherini

Leila and Kelly perform a skit called "All Aboard the
Ally Ship"

Intermission

50/50 raffle drawing (Leila and Kelly)

Roberto plays "Asturias" on acoustic guitar

Chris reads his poem called "Puzzles in the Road"

Mika and Talia sing and dance to "Can't Stop Me"
by Angie T

Rick spins quarters

Seeley and Trish sing "My Girl" by The Temptations

Yaya leads cast and crew in "We Are All Beautiful"
by Miss Kris

Emcee: Melissa

Stage Manager: Ellie

Stagehands: Ronnie, Kadyn, and Brinley

Program Design and Script: Sam and Tracey

Tickets: Mr. Sydney and Minh

Raffle: Leila and Kelly

Video Recording: Mason

AUTHOR'S NOTE

Language is changing swiftly around us, especially for the QUILTBAG+ community. I'm not a historian, but I'd like to provide at least a little context here for some of the language that has been used to refer to people who are not straight (attracted to the opposite sex) and cisgender (gender matches the one assigned at birth). Only fifty years ago, people generally spoke of the *gay* community, or the *gay and lesbian* community, since *gay*, a word to describe people who are attracted to the same sex, often refers only to men. *Lesbian* describes women who are attracted to other women. In the 1970s and 1980s, *bisexual* people, who are attracted to more than one gender, called for visibility, and by the 1990s, many people and organizations spoke of the *lesbian*, *gay*, and *bisexual* (LGB) community.

Over the last twenty years or so, especially in the last five to ten, more and more people and groups have recognized that when we talk about our community, we need to acknowledge *transgender* folks (whose gender doesn't match their gender as assigned at birth), *intersex* people (who are born with, or later develop, sex characteristics that do not fit traditional definitions of male or female bodies), *asexual* individuals (who are not attracted to anyone, or only in specific situations), and *pansexual* people (who are attracted to many genders). Around the same time, many activists reclaimed *queer* as a more radical way of talking about our community, especially by people who didn't want to fit in with straight culture. They took a word that had been used as an insult against them and turned it into a label of pride. While it has become a primary identity for some, others don't like the word because of its history.

That doesn't mean that TQIAP+ folks are new to the

LGB community, but that we as a culture are learning more comprehensive ways to talk about ourselves. And there's more language to come. The question becomes: How do we talk about our community in ways that are both aware of the value of commonly understood language and respectful to people who deserve to have language that works for them?

The most common acronym these days to represent this range is LGBTQIAP+ (Lesbian Gay Bisexual Transgender Queer Intersex Asexual Pansexual and more). The plus sign acknowledges that our understanding of sexuality is growing, and that many people use other language to describe themselves. I've also used the term QUILTBAG+ (Queer Unsure Intersex Lesbian Transgender Bisexual Asexual Gay and more) in this book, as coined by feminist artist Sadie Lee in 2006. I appreciate how easy it is to say, as well as the quilt imagery. We are a community of disparate people who come together to create something beautiful, and the reference to the AIDS Quilt is worth noting. However, I don't think QUILTBAG+ is perfect—I wish it included pansexuality, and some people don't like the *-bag* ending. I hope that I have done justice to the real-life process of developing language in the way I represent the Rainbow Spectrum's conversations. And I look forward to what comes next as we continue to refine language to meet our needs.

If you've been thinking about your own gender and/or sexuality, you can research online for terms that might help you put a name to how you're feeling. And if you don't know how you're feeling, there's language for that too—questioning and being unsure are real parts of life, especially if you might not be straight or cisgender. You might face some tough times if you haven't already, so set yourself up with a support network of people you know you can talk to—whether that's your friends, family, teachers, or someone else you trust to listen and to support you. At the same time, you don't need to share your feelings with anyone you don't want to.

Know that there are resources out there for you. Many cities and towns have local community centers, and growing numbers of middle and elementary schools are developing groups like the Rainbow Spectrum. The Trevor Project, an amazing organization for LGBTQIAP+ folks under twenty-five, has the TrevorLifeline (866-488-7386), support by text (text START to 678678), and TrevorChat (thetrevorproject.org), where you can talk with a counselor 24/7. Please, if you need help, reach out. And if you're not sure if it's for you—it is! We need you around.

Thanks for reading and for being yourself.

ACKNOWLEDGMENTS

Supreme thanks to my phenomenal editor, David Levithan, for the vision, support, and careful critique that have now brought us through three books. May there be many more to come. And matching appreciation for my stupendous agent, Jenn Laughran, whose brand of snarky sincerity has guided me through the bizarre waters of publishing like some sort of Disney talking-compass character. Much gratitude to everyone at Scholastic, especially Maeve Norton for another amazing cover, Lauren Donovan, Emily Heddleson, Maya Marlette, Lizette Serrano, Tracy van Straaten, the amazing team of sales reps, and anyone who has ever helped me navigate a Scholastic elevator.

Great appreciation for the young people at schools, libraries, and groups around the country who have let me into their spaces over the last few years to talk about being young and QUILTBAG+. Special thanks to the groups and individuals who workshopped this book with me for language and representation: Rachel Williams and the other amazing students of the GSA at Bret Harte Middle School in Oakland; Joao Santos; Avelina Santos; Cayden Lewis-McCabe; Devin Harkness and the fantastic middle school students of SAGA at ACCESS Academy in Portland, Oregon; and Sarah Goldman and the fabulous fifth-grade students of Queen Anne Elementary in Seattle. Thanks also to grown-up librarian, author, and friend, Kyle Lukoff, for his spot-on critique.

Deepest thanks to my We Need Diverse Books mentees, Kaija Langley (2018) and medina (2019), for helping me learn more about my writing by exploring yours with you, and for the future pleasure of your books in the world. I'm excited to be peers with you.

And then, of course, there are the people in my life who make it special. My days and life have been and continue to be enriched by the friendship, love, and company of people like Jay Williams, Jean Marie Stine, Timnah Steinman, tee Silverstein, Beth Kelly, Alanna Kelly, Mike Jung, Frankie Hill, Jen Herrington, Robin Bowen, Amy Benson, and Blake C. Aarens. Massive love for my dear Miss Holly and my outstanding roommate, Rebecca Cobre. And endless love and appreciation for my parents, Steve and Cindy Gino; my sister, Robin Gridgeman; and her kids, Kadyn and Brinley.

No list can properly encompass the scope of the process from an author's brain nugget to a reader reaching the acknowledgments page, and yet, here I am, trying again to turn a dynamic process into a static list. My apologies if I haven't included you here. I do love you.